BESIDE

— THE —

LONG

RIVER

LOUELLA
BRYANT

Black Rose Writing | Texas

ISBN: 978-1-68433-855-9
PUBLISHED BY BLACK ROSE WRITING
www.blackrosewriting.com

Printed in the United States of America
Suggested Retail Price (SRP) $18.95

Beside the Long River is printed in Book Antiqua

*As a planet-friendly publisher, Black Rose Writing does its best to eliminate
unnecessary waste to reduce paper usage and energy costs, while never
compromising the reading experience. As a result, the final word count vs.
page count may not meet common expectations.

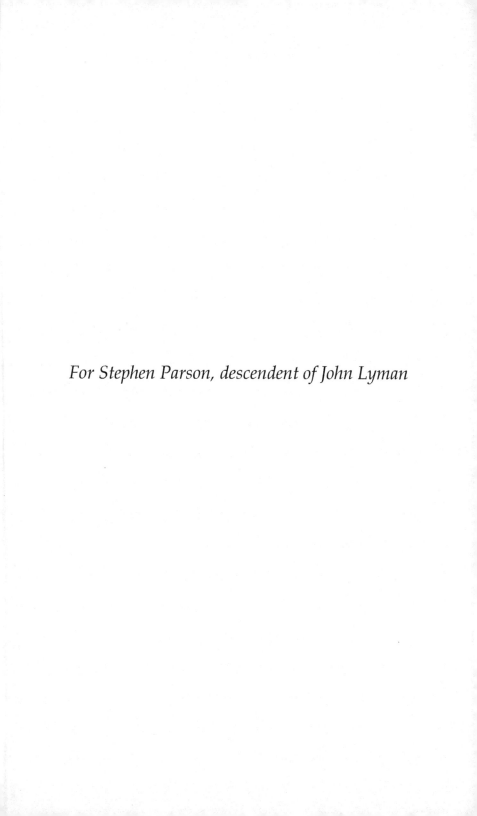

For Stephen Parson, descendent of John Lyman

CONTENTS

BESIDE

— THE —

LONG
RIVER

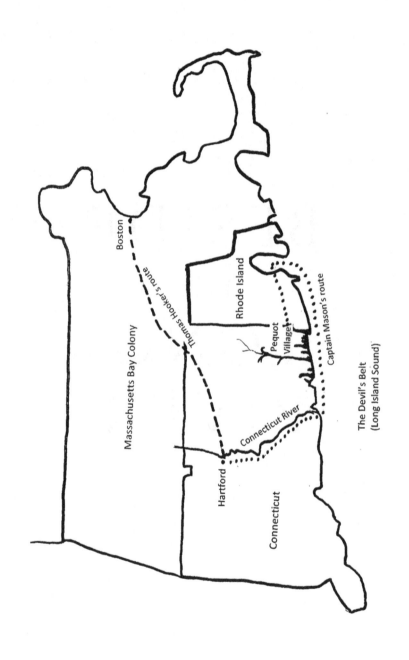

Boston

Thomas Hooker's route

Massachusetts Bay Colony

Rhode Island

Pequot Village

Captain Mason's route

Connecticut River

Hartford

Connecticut

The Devil's Belt
(Long Island Sound)

THE FIRST FAREWELL

"**I** won't go, Papa. I won't!" I stamped my foot and squeezed my hands into fists.

"We're to board the ship *Lyon* tomorrow morning, Sarah," my father said. "You wouldn't want to be left behind, would you?"

"I'll lock myself in the fruit bin. I will!"

Papa leaned forward in his rocking chair and glared at me. He was a patient man, but I know I tried his tolerance.

"Don't be imprudent. How would a twelve-year-old girl provide for herself?"

"I'll—I'll live with Lizzy, that's what." Lizzy was my best friend. If I crossed a vast ocean, I'd surely never see her again.

A frown lined Papa's forehead. He was losing patience with me.

"The Massachusetts Bay colony will be an example to the world for religious freedom. We'll live among hundreds of other Puritans."

"What about your business, Papa? Are we to be poor?" He was a wizard with numbers and so successful managing accounts that our family lived in a big house with hired servants to work for us. I had lacked for nothing. The prospect of giving up my comforts was unbearable.

"You leave business to me. We are all going to America — you, your sister, your two brothers, your mother, and I. And that's that."

Papa was an old man. I wasn't sure he could survive an ocean voyage, much less the hardships of setting up a household in a wilderness. Who knew what would greet us thousands of miles away in a land the English had colonized at Plymouth Plantation a dozen years ago? Would there be shops? Bakeries? Even a tearoom?

My pleading wasn't working, so I tried another tactic.

"Lizzy says there are giants and fiends of every sort. What do you know about America any more than you know about a distant star?"

"Sarah, the Massachusetts colony has been in existence for two years, and I have not heard a single report of fiends or giants."

I choked back tears. "But why, Papa? Why must we go?"

He heaved a sigh and studied his hands. "It goes hard here in England for the Puritans, even in our own Ongar Parrish. If we stay, I can't predict what will happen to us. America will give us a fresh beginning. We have no choice, daughter." He regarded me from under his bushy brows. "Now, be sure your things are packed for boarding the ship at sunrise."

I had an inkling of what Papa meant by "goes hard." I had witnessed a Quaker with a bandage on his head from having part of an ear sliced off for some offense. A man was locked in the bilbo, an iron bar with shackles attached to his ankles. Others took their punishment in the stocks or were whipped with knotted cords for the crime of drunkenness. My father liked a cider in the evening, but he practiced moderation. I could not have endured seeing him suffer such a punishment. Women were not excused from penalties either. One walked the streets wearing the letter B sewn to the front of her dress for speaking blasphemy. I would like to have known what obscenity had passed her lips because I often felt a curse on my own.

We Puritans always had to be mindful of our actions. My teacher kept a whispering stick in the classroom corner which she once used on Lizzy. I told the teacher if she struck Lizzy, she'd also have to strike me since I was the recipient of Lizzy's secrets. My hands were red for days afterward. Punishments were inflicted to make examples of the offenders so others would practice righteous behavior. The magistrates judged who was righteous and who was not, and I believed their judgment depended on their daily whims.

I took great risk in arguing with Papa. Women were commanded to be obedient to husbands and children to parents. We were not to have opinions of our own. The penalty would be administered by Papa. I was fortunate not only that he had not raised a paddle to me, but his forbearance saved me from having to eat in a standing position for a day or two.

When it appeared I would not dissuade Papa from his vision of America as our salvation, I spun around and dashed out the door, lifting my skirt as I ran through the wildflowers in the meadow. Lizzy would wait under the tree, the one where we sat and wove flowers in our hair. And such hair Lizzy had—coils of red her cap could not contain. She said her hair came from the flames of hell, which was where she'd end up for reading the likes of William Shakespeare and Geoffrey Chaucer. Lizzy kept the volumes in the hayloft, and we read aloud to each other in dim light filtering through the barn boards. Papa said Lizzy must have a touch of Scot in her because of her crimson hair. But the Scottish were Catholic and Lizzy was a Puritan, like me. We could have been better in our conduct, but we endured the scoldings of our fathers and repented at Sunday services. Surely that was worth one small corner of heaven.

Lizzy knew of our voyage but not that the ship would sail so soon. When I told her, she made up a song for me.

Beans and barley, rice and curds —
Think on me and say these words
And I'll be there as thin as air
Plaiting flowers in your hair.

As she sang the line about being *as thin as air*, it dawned on me how much air would separate us when I sailed away. Just before we parted, she leaned over and clawed a handful of English soil. Then she pulled open my apron pocket and sprinkled in the rich black dirt.

"So you won't forget," she said.

"As if I could forget," I told her.

"And take this with you." She handed me a package covered in heavy paper. "Keep it hidden and don't open it until you get on the ship."

Before we parted, I hugged her hard one last time. Oh my sweet Lizzy, never could I have imagined how agonizing a goodbye could be. If only I had known that this was the first goodbye of many I would grieve in the coming years.

That night, I packed all I could into a satchel, including pen, ink, and paper so I could keep a record of my new life. If I was going to be part of history, I wanted someone to read about it in the future—provided I survived. Then I lit the last stub of a candle by my bed. Not wanting to wait another minute, I uncovered Lizzy's parting gift. She had passed her copy of Chaucer's *Canterbury Tales* to me. Now I would have something other than needlework to pass the weeks of travel—so long as I could keep the book hidden.

I opened to The Knight's Tale and read: *Naught may the woful spirit in myn hearte Declare a point of alle my sorwes smerte.* The words were hard to decipher two hundred years after Chaucer wrote them. He left out letters for some words and added letters to others. "Woful" must have been "woeful," and "alle," was surely "all." What was "sorwes"? If I said the word aloud, it sounded like "sorrows." But what did *smerte* mean? To smart meant to hurt, probably spelled differently in Chaucer's day.

Canterbury Tales was like a foreign language but if I kept reading, his meaning would be easier to grasp. Chaucer seemed to understand my deepest feelings. My spirit that night was indeed woeful and sorrowful, and my heart smerte more than ever I could remember.

Before I took to sleep, I buried Chaucer deep in my satchel where Father would not find it.

BRISTOL WHARF

Ghostly fog hung over the bay when we arrived at the harbor. Tied to the dock, the *Lyon* nodded in the water like a lazy sea monster. Three masts spiked into the cloud around which gulls flapped and screeched. Women chattered with each other or called out to squealing children. Sailors barked orders for passengers to stow their possessions as they dragged their trunks and furniture over the gangway. Water slapped the ship's hull, and a clanging bell marked time as I would mark the coming weeks. In the damp air, I sensed excitement mixed with nervousness. For me there was only gloom.

While Papa spoke with the captain, my brother Richard squinted toward the *Lyon's* stern.

"See this schooner, Sarah? She's over a hundred feet from bowsprit to back rail. Well-caulked, too, and seaworthy."

"The ship is a woman? Then I have faith she will carry us to America safely." I had that dim hope, at least.

"A cannonball from a Dunkirk pirate would do her in." Richard planted a fist on his hip.

"Pirates? Honestly, Richard, I'm not a child. It's 1632 — there will be no pirates on our route." I was nearly thirteen. When would my brother think of me as grown up?

Richard laughed. "Don't worry—the *Lyon* is spry enough to outrun them. This will be her third voyage across the Atlantic."

My elder brother was sixteen and knew so many facts that I wondered at the size of his brain. "And if we don't outrun the pirates—" He pointed to black iron barrels sticking through portholes in the hull. "Those cannon can send a three-pound shot two thousand feet."

Cannon fire, pirates, storms—what had Papa got us into?

"How soon does the fighting start?" John burst out. He was nine years of age and as bothersome as a mosquito.

Richard checked the sky. "Pirates attack under cover of night and the sooner we make way, the safer we'll be. Best get our things onto the ship. Be hasty now."

John was more likely to believe Richard's tall tales. It was boredom that concerned me.

Richard untied sacks from our wagon and set them on the ground.

"Help me get these goods aboard the *Lyon*, John," he said.

"A lion that swims," John scoffed. "Sea lion would be a better name."

"Haven't you heard of sea lions?" I cuffed his ear playfully. "Those fat creatures could eat a boy like you in one gulp." I plopped a sack onto his shoulder. "And if you give me any trouble, you might just end up breakfast for one of those whiskered giants."

"Go on," John said. "We'll see who goes overboard first." He shrugged off the sack.

"We'll have no talk of going overboard." As usual, Papa ended the argument.

"Take that sack aboard, John." I picked it up and balanced it again on his shoulder.

"But I'm just a boy," he complained.

"A whining boy at that." I patted his cap. "But strong as a sea lion, if I'm not mistaken."

Richard pushed a wooden bucket toward him. "And you can carry the slop bucket, too."

"Slop bucket?"

"Where did you expect we'd do our necessaries for the next three months?"

From the look on his face, I suspected John had given no thought to necessaries.

"Three months? Three whole months?"

"It's a wide sea, brother," I said. "And if the wind fails to cooperate, we may be on the ship longer. Now what do you think about necessaries?"

"There's a whole ocean I can shite in," he said.

I laughed. "That's a balancing act I'd like to see."

As passengers made their way onto the ship, I wondered whether any felt the dread that hovered over me. For most of them, the *Lyon* was their escape. For me, it was a prison sentence. So much time confined to the decks of a wooden cell gave me no promise of a better life. Whether I agreed or not, I was being ripped from the only home I knew.

While I watched travelers lead their cows and oxen over the gangway, I was vexed with Papa for selling our workhorse Lofty. She was a gentle soul for being so strong in the harness, and she nuzzled me when I brushed her. But Papa said a horse was too skittish for the rolling of the boat. Ruby was more sure-footed and we would need the ox to pull the plow.

"Phillip, come back!" a woman called. Her little boy had broken away from her and dashed up the gangway. A sailor caught the tyke and hauled him to his mother. She thanked him and said, "My son doesn't lack for enthusiasm. I'll do my best to keep him quiet during the voyage."

The sailor winked. "The sea, she will not mind some noise." I recognized his French accent from visitors I had heard in Ongar Parrish. His eyes were kind, which gave me hope. For such a long sail, we would need all the kindness we could muster for each other.

When all passengers finally were settled aboard, the dock workers untied lines from cleats and the crew raised the sails. *I lay Redy to wenden on my pilgrimage*, Chaucer wrote. But I was not ready — I would never be ready. But I couldn't stop the sails from lifting up the masts like square clouds — four at first and then three more when we were away from the harbor. It was a magnificent sight, I had to admit. Nothing but cloth pulling forward a ship of one hundred twenty-three people — fifty of them children — livestock, furniture, and provisions to last for a dozen weeks.

Overhead, gulls circled, squealing spiral songs around the tip of the mast as the land sped away from us. First the houses along the inlet, then trees and rocky crags all rushed back toward the pebbly beaches of my beloved England. Within minutes, the great island became a thin line along the horizon. And when the *Lyon* sailed over the curve of earth, my homeland lingered on the water a moment longer and then sank into the sea.

Oh, Lizzy, are you thinking of me as I am you? I missed the hours we spent in our hideaway under the orchard's leaves where we shared our secrets. Lizzy wanted to be a midwife, and I had fantasies of writing adventures and romances and tawdry tales. Her family hadn't the money to sail to Massachusetts, but I knew one day she would come. Until then, I vowed not to take another best friend, no matter how lonely I became.

Would I be an old woman before we reached the other shore? Thirteen was an in-between age—neither here nor there. My body was changing daily. One moment I was as giddy as a spring daffodil and the next I fought back tears. My own thoughts confused me. I had no one to talk to about these things. My sister Phillis was engrossed with finding a husband, and Mother had too many tasks to listen to my complaints. So I dangled like a worm from a silken thread, blown by breezes, anchored nowhere.

Finally, a single bird followed the *Lyon*, shrieking as if calling me back. But I could not go back. My only possibility was to go forward—to what I didn't know.

RATS

Because there was nothing but water ahead of the ship's bow, I investigated the planks of wood holding me above the whales and sharks. The *Lyon* had four levels, the lowest a hold for storing chicken cages, livestock and feed. I was blessed — or maybe cursed — with an acute sense of smell. Therefore, it should not be surprising that I did not relish going below for my turn feeding the animals and shoveling their waste into buckets which I hauled to the top deck and heaved overboard. I thought instead of nicer aromas. Lizzy had a perfume of wild strawberries. My sister Phillis smelled of bread dough, no matter her humor, and I often thought baking her would improve her temperament. Molasses and herbs wafted from my mother, and John carried the essence of grass bending in a stiff wind. Richard's scent was of heated iron, as of a musket lately fired. Papa smelled clean, like soap lathered with justice and goodness. If I were blind, I'd could identify my family by their aromas.

We hung our hammocks above the hold where the stale air reeked of whatever fetidness lingered from the previous voyage — animal dung, vomit, piss, sweat, and — oddly — the faint and acidic scent of lemon. No potpourri of dried lavender disguised the foul fragrances. I supposed that either the west winds would blow the stink away or I would get used to it, and I set to work making my bed, tying my hammock between two of the ship's support posts. Phillis had more trouble with hers. One end was shy of a beam.

"*Un peu plus de corde, oui?*" It was the sailor who had caught young Phillip. He pulled some rope from a pocket and knotted it to my sister's hammock.

"I can manage," she snapped. Why did Phillis have to be so unfriendly? It was no wonder that at nineteen she was still unwed.

The sailor gave a playful salute. "Call on Frenchie if ye need help — *c'est moi.*" His fingers brushed Phillis's wrist when he pressed the hemp rope into her hand. She jerked away and mumbled to herself. She would do well to be wary of him. Likely he was not Puritan, and I could not envision Phillis as a seaman's wife. In fact, she hadn't a single prospect for marriage. In England she had deemed all Puritan bachelors dreadfully ugly, unbearably dull, or widowed and far too old. She wanted someone pious and with means to support her. She also wanted him to have a comely face and not gangly like a narrow-chested schoolteacher. She would have liked the squire of Chaucer's Knight, *A lovyere, and a lusty bachelor, With lokkes cruller, as they were leyd in press.* A curly-haired lover of twenty years would have done her well, especially one robust and *of greet strengthe.* But a woman of her years could not afford to be particular, especially with her straight hair, nose a trifle too generous, and a shadow of dark fuzz on her upper lip. She had precious few years left before the vultures of age scratched their marks along her face. Even Lizzy's sister, just fourteen, was betrothed. As for me, my sling of canvas had just enough space for one, and I vowed to remain single as did Emilia in The Knight's Tale when she swore to Diana to be a maiden all her life. *Ne never wol I be no love ne wyf.* Being a house drudge might have been enough for Phillis, but my ambitions reached higher than wifely duties.

The hammock rocked as the ship rose and fell over the waves. Surrounded by mothers and babies, I felt swaddled in a cradle. Phillis says I entered life in the midst of a storm, wailing so loudly that she worried I might be the devil's offspring. I often wondered that myself, but I was sure there was a special destiny awaiting me in America. Whether good or ill, I could not yet tell.

During the night I felt a splinter press into my cheek. In the pitch blackness I heard something scratching and skittering nearby. Whatever it was gave off a rank odor. I pressed down with my hands and felt rough planks beneath my palms.

"What in heaven's name —?" Phillis said.

I sat up, dizzy and nauseous, my bladder aching for relief.

"Get up off the floor," Phillis commanded, "before the rats make a midnight snack of you."

I pushed myself to my knees. "Mice, you mean?"

"Rats," she said. "The size of cats. Have you not heard them?"

I had a horror of rodents, the scavengers who stole bread from our house in Ongar Parrish unless I hid it under a tin. Better to eat an entire loaf rather than leave a crumb for the vile creatures. I hated their pointy noses, their quivering whiskers, and their eyes like drips of filthy oil.

"Why do you think your bed is a hammock instead of a pallet on the floor where the vermin would scamper over you all night?" Phillis said. "And, speaking of floor, what might you be doing down there?"

"Oh," I said, "the ship must have listed."

"And you listed with it. Get back in your sling—there's hours yet before the sun."

Hours, I thought, and my bladder near to bursting. In the dark I would never find the slop bucket, so I crawled into my bed and lay awake. Grasping the hammock in each hand, I concentrated on staying afloat in my ship of cloth.

"Tomorrow," Phillis said, her voice full of sleep, "we'll get John to track down your rat."

"Likely as not he'll skewer it and roast it for our lunch," I answered.

"Hush," said Phillis. "Good night now, and sweet dreams."

THE FIRST DEATH

In the following days I became a mermaid. My world was watery green. Mother and Phyllis washed clothes in saltwater and waited for rain to rinse them. They helped the other women prepare the two daily meals, such as they were. For breakfast, brine flavored my porridge and at mid-day I stomached a stew of fish caught by a crewman's hook. If the fish were not taking the hook, in the evening we had barley. A gift of some poor sea creature was cause for prayers of thanks, and I sucked the bones of mackerel or herring and considered myself fortunate. Between the meager meals, I feasted on wind and light and imagined myself riding upon a whale's back. The undersea surely held more adventure than the *Lyon's* tiny buoyant world.

In Ongar Parrish it would be harvest time by now. The pears would be ripe, and I longed for their sweet juice to drip down my chin while I watched our workmen cut the wheat. But what did it matter? English wheat was no longer my concern. For now, I had nothing to do but feed Ruby and keep an eye on Papa. He had no appetite and was growing thinner by the day. He often gave Richard his portion at meals. Richard never refused, gorging himself like a caterpillar making ready for its long sleep in the cocoon. We were all like caterpillars, wrapped in a chrysalis of wood, waiting for our transformation in the New World.

Mother had packed a bureau handed down from my grandmother, a large trunk of clothing and bedding, burlap bags of kitchen and garden tools, and a box of dried herbs. They would be our first furnishings in the New World. A pouch of flower seeds would make pretty gardens. Candlesticks and beeswax candles, cups, plates, and knives were packed in a box along with a pewter pitcher with an unfortunate dent where my brother John had knocked it from the shelf while swashbuckling with one of his imaginary pirates. Papa had sold our other possessions or left them for our home's new owner.

How I missed the aromas of England thick with horses, sweet with hay, and salty with zephyrs drifting inland from the sea. Our house was no mansion, that was sure, but the roof kept out the rain and the inside was always clean, thanks to my chafed knuckles. Our workmen had pruned the trees last season, and now they were heavy with apples and pears ripe for picking. There would be no warm pie this fall, no fruit sauce or dried apple leather to chew through the winter. Often I lifted my apron to my nose and breathed the perfume of England.

The *Lyon* was larger than the Mayflower, the first ship to sail into Massachusetts Bay, but we still were crowded. How can one feel suffocated when blown by the wind under a boundless sky? Yet, I felt I could hardly draw a deep breath. In my most restless moments, I pretended the sea was a magic carpet transporting me high above green clouds capped with foam, and at other times it was a roadway alive with dolphins leaping like hares in our path. Or the ocean's surface was a desert, one desolate dune following another and rolling off the brink of the world.

High above the deck, the sails billowed like giant's laundry. Once in a while a sail got caught on a rigging and sailors had to climb ratline ladders to free the cloth. Like spiders, they worked their way aloft and then sidled along the yardarms to loose or gather a thousand square feet of flapping canvas as the ship swayed and dipped into billow valleys. There was nothing except a keen sense of balance keeping the men from tumbling either onto the *Lyon's* deck or into the sea. When Captain Pierce called "Mainsail haul!" we zigged or zagged against the current so that it seemed we had to sail twice the distance a straight line would have taken us. In rough wind, waves washed over the gunwales, and when rain caught me on the upper deck, the droplets pelted like needles. In this way, we made slow progress.

I was leaning on the railing one afternoon watching water spume from the ship's hull when John came up next to me.

"What do you think is on the sea bottom?" he asked.

"Shells and fish. Maybe wrecks of ships sunk by storms," I said.

"I'd guess carcasses of men who walked the pirates' planks." He leaned over the railing and spat, then reached down and scratched his ankle.

"You have fleas?" I asked. Rats must have carried the vermin aboard. My legs had scabs where I'd scratched until I bled. At least the fleas were eating well.

John ignored the fleas as he ignored my question.

"I'm watching for pirates."

"Would you know a pirate if you met one?"

"Yea—the captain wears a patch where he lost an eye in a sword fight, and he clumps on an ivory leg. He's got on a three-pointed hat, a red sash across his chest, and a saber at his side."

"And you'll be ready for a skirmish, I suppose?"

"Get me a sword and I'll show him a fight."

John needed a distraction from boredom. I had needlework when my fingers were warm enough and Chaucer's stories if there was sufficient light, but the ship's churning made my stomach queasy and words floated on the page as I read. Instead, I pretended I was part of an Indian camp where native women tanned hides, built fires to roast meat, decorated their clothing with feathers, and chanted songs to their children. If my imagination wore out, I chewed my cuticles and counted rodent droppings scattered across the deck. But what was John to do? He couldn't climb the rope ladder without a crew member plucking him off.

"Break your derriere, ye will," Frenchie said when once he'd gotten a few feet above decks. If Frenchie turned his back, John would have climbed to the owl's nest.

"Of course, when you capture a pirate you'll be merciful, won't you?" I said, playing along with his fantasy.

"Captain Montrose has seventeen notches on his belt," John said. "One for each of the Englishmen he's skewered. But yes, I'll feed them to the sharks rather than run them through."

Frenchie overheard John's daydream. "What sort of weapon are ye fancying?"

John looked at shoes and mumbled, "Sword, sir."

Frenchie frowned down at him. "You'll need a grand one for the likes of the rogues you'll be sparring with."

A wooden rod leaned against a compartment door, and Frenchie picked it up.

"The blade broke clean off this axe handle. Had to shape a new one," he said. "No sense wasting the old one, though, if you can put it to some use, *oui*?" He offered John the axe handle, worn from many hands chopping who knew what.

John ran his palm over the wood and beamed his thanks. The seaman tousled the boy's hair and went back to work. John stuck his new sword in his belt and its weight pulled him to one side. When he drew it out, a rough place caught in the cloth of his knickers. He drew it again, more careful this time, and jabbed with the gusto of a saber that had a glistening hilt burnished and carved with scenes of heroic battles.

"A brave Theseus you are, little brother," I said, "with your fine stick of wood."

"Sword," he corrected, stabbing me with a sharp glance.

"A brainless sword, then." There was evil in me to tease my brother so.

"When we see pirates, I'll show you who's brainless," he said.

We had seen no sign of pirates or any other vessels, and I left John to his phantom enemies.

The passage was hardest for the youngsters. Penned up like sheep, they yowled and squirmed. Mothers held to their daughters' dresses and used straps to anchor their sons from toddling to the gunwale where they might tempt the sea. I could hardly concentrate on my lesson books for all the noise.

The racket must have bothered Frenchie, too. One windy day when the *Lyon* made steady headway, he strung a length of rope between the mainmast and a second mast. One by one, he took each child by the hand and squeezed a little fist around the stretched rope.

"Here ye are now, *mes amis*," he said. "Take hold of this line and ye can do a jig if ye care to. Just don't let go, or else ye'll end up in the drink."

For an hour the children kicked and hopped and walked hand over hand along the rope and back again, like colorful flags on a line. Even Mother laughed for the first time since the voyage began.

Four-year-old Phillip was in high spirits. John tapped his sword on the deck and said, "Dance, Phillip, dance!" The boy waved his cap with his free hand and kicked up his heels in a silly prance.

When the wind swirled, Captain Pierce ordered the children to stay close by their parents until the weather calmed. The youngsters bawled in protest. Captain Pierce was strict, but he had a soft spot for children.

"Well," he said. "Five minutes more. But watch yourselves and when I give the call, it's below decks with you."

The ship rocked and the children staggered and tripped. Mothers called for them to hold on. The more the deck rocked, the more Phillip made funny faces and gave his audience some fancy footwork, his shirt flying out like a bird's wings.

The masts creaked against the force of the wind, and the ship became a stallion galloping over hills of water. "Children below!" Captain Pierce yelled. "Quickly now!"

Women grabbed for the little ones, but Phillip dodged his mother and ran the width of the deck. As the ship rolled, the boy slipped to the starboard rail, just meters from the water's spray. A look of glee still on his face, he flapped his hat clownishly as his feet flew up from under him.

I half expected Phillip to take flight like the gulls at Bristol harbor. But instead of winging, he slid between the spindles.

Without thinking, I bolted across the deck and wrenched my hand around one short arm, thin as a fish bone. The boy's small feet kicked the air, dancing as he had done on the deck. The weight of such a compact bundle surprised me—he seemed solid as iron. It was as if he had swallowed sinkers to weigh so heavy. The cloth of his shirt was coarse and felt like sand. And just like sand, it began to sift through my fingers.

Someone howled, "Hold on!"

I did hold on. I would have held on forever if I'd had to. I clenched the wrist with all my strength and prayed that the wrist would stay attached to the arm, the arm to the shoulder, the shoulder to the boy. My only thought was not to let go, even though his skin was slippery with salt water—not to let go, not even when a wave reached up like a wet tongue and licked the child as a dog might lick a flea. But the sea's hunger was stronger than my will, and a second wave pulled Phillip from my grip. His white shirt flashed, and he disappeared into the great throat of the ocean.

The gray hat floated for one blink of an eye and then drifted away behind the ship.

Someone pulled my ankles, and then the deck was beneath me again. Richard shoved me aside and swung a leg over the rail. As he was about to take off like some long-legged crane, I thought how he couldn't swim, how we would lose him, too. In that moment I called on any power to save my brother, be it providence or grace. But it was Frenchie who answered.

The sailor clasped Richard by the arm and hauled him back to safety.

"Turn the ship!" I shouted.

"We cannot," Frenchy said. He looked at me with eyes glossy with tears. "You're not at fault, *ma chère*. The ship already is beyond where the boy fell." He gulped a breath that was almost a sob and cried, "*Le garçon est mort.*"

There was a cry, and if Frenchie hadn't grabbed her, the boy's mother would have flung herself over the side to follow her son. She fought Frenchie, matching his strength, but he held on and wrestled her from the railing, from the hungry sea.

That evening Reverend Eliot delivered a eulogy and asked us all to pray for the young soul. I prayed the best I could, but what was the use? Phillip's soul was no doubt already in heaven. Later, I stood at the stern with John. He took the saber from his belt and ran his hand down the hilt. Without a word, he drew the wood back and flung it. The axe handle spun and twirled, but before his sword found the sea, my young brother had already turned away.

THE ARRIVAL

I, that am exyled and bareyne Of alle grace, and in so greet despair That ther nis erthe, water, fyr, ne eir. Like Chaucer's Knight, I, too, was exiled, barren of Puritan grace, and despairing of hope that what lay ahead was any better than what lay behind. But the Knight was mistaken— aboard the *Lyon* there was air and water aplenty but no fire and certainly no earth in this watery universe. I was left to my thoughts, which were as dark as louse nits.

Some days when the wind was still, the *Lyon* drifted idly and the sailors cursed the sky. Other days we heeled over mountainous waves in such ferocious storms that at night my hammock swung like a pendulum and I feared we might all perish at sea before ever setting foot on solid ground.

By the time October's chill bit my cheeks, we were each in desperate need of fresh water baths. The older passengers complained of stiffness from sitting. Papa rubbed his knees. His face was pale, even under the sun's unblinking eye.

"Are you all right, Papa?" I should have addressed him as "my lord," which was more respectful, but since I was a little girl toddling about, he had not rebuked me for calling him by the more familiar name.

"Never worry—" He tried for a pleasant expression but winced instead.

Frenchie held out a jar of yellow half-moons. "These will grease your joints."

"What is it?" I asked.

"*Citron.* Chew the rind and you'll feel better tomorrow."

He handed a slice to me and one to Papa.

"In France we have a drink called *limonade,*" Frenchie said. "Squeeze the juice and add sugar from West Indies cane. None better—save with a splash of spirits."

Other than the health benefits of beer or cider, Papa was not given to strong drink, but I'd have taken Frenchie's exotic nectar, spirits or no. The lemon was bitter, but I pretended it was sweet sunshine and let the juice flow down my throat.

Between Frenchie's lemons and the dried vervain herb Mother had me chew, I was feeling well but my dreams were of roasted mutton and tarts slathered with thick cream. Heaven would have to forgive the growling of my ungrateful stomach.

How many days had we been at sea? Seventy? Eighty? I'd lost count. If my father had named me Patience, I might have been better able to endure the endless journey.

Because of the wind, I kept below decks much of the time. Either I lost myself in Chaucer or stared at the floorboards, marveling that only a few planks held me above the sharks that would make a supper of me. My very life was in the hands of boat builders.

On a gray November day, I wrapped my cloak about me and came to the deck for fresh air. As I stood at the bow, a white feather fluttered down upon my arm. Overhead, birds squealed and darted around the ship's mast.

Feathers? Birds? Oh, glory be!

"Land ho!" a crewman shouted from atop the crow's nest.

"On deck, men!" the captain called. He peered through his scope over the bowsprit.

"Have we come to Boston?" I asked. With my naked eye there looked to be nothing but barren beach.

"We've gone too far south," Captain Pierce said. "We'll anchor here and tomorrow we'll round Cape Cod into Massachusetts Bay."

"But—" I started to protest. I didn't want to waste another hour on the cursed ship.

The captain winked at me. "I'm sure you can make do with one more night."

I supposed the captain was right. One more night wouldn't make much difference.

At daybreak Captain Pierce hoisted anchor and set the bow into the wind. The sight of land off the port side was nothing but that—land. Not a human or animal in sight. I dearly hoped to find some sort of civilization in Massachusetts Bay.

We rounded the cape's tip and cruised past sand dunes into harbor. Captain Pierce saluted our arrival with a thunderous report from the ship's cannon—the most joyful, promising thunder I'd heard in weeks.

The peal of church bells welcomed us. As we sailed near the shore, I saw an odd-looking town perched by the bay. Village streets crawled with activity, oxen drawing carts, women toting bundles, children clutching their mothers' skirts. Villagers stopped their business and waved their arms. Outside the crowd, dark-haired people wrapped in animal furs watched with round-eyed children. The natives were not as I had imagined. Nothing looked recognizable. What was this wild place?

The crewmen dropped anchor, and Frenchy helped us family by family into a skiff and ferried us to shore. The air was perfumed with pine, smoke and earth, but my heart pounded with anticipation. Although what awaited me was a mystery, I was ready for anything and gladly stepped from the awful, stinking ship.

A slender man with sad eyes and a neat, pointed beard opened his arms toward us.

"Welcome to Massachusetts, friends!"

The captain shook his hand. "It was a fine voyage, Governor Winthrop."

The governor ordered fires to be lit and meat skewered for roasting. Tables were brought from houses, and Governor Winthrop declared a day of thanksgiving. In a short while, I was feasting on proper food, my first in three months—breads, cooked pumpkin, and roasted turkey. There were offerings from the sea, too—oysters, mussels and fish. I found the eel spicy and tough and the bubbly cider made my head spin, but I filled myself as if I would never eat again.

"Where will we live, Papa?" I asked. He had been speaking with townsfolk.

"Empty houses are scarce, but I'm told a few were left by settlers who decided the Massachusetts Bay colony was not their cup of tea and sailed back to England. There's a vacant house in Charlestown, a short walk from the village."

After we had eaten, Papa led us to the structure, which was large—at least by the *Lyon's* standards—with sleeping quarters upstairs.

"Why has no one taken this house?" Mother asked.

Papa hesitated. "In truth, the occupants died of smallpox," he said. "No one wants the risk of catching the disease." He looked at his four children. "But we're a healthy lot, are we not?"

Smallpox had taken tens of thousands of lives in England, Europe and even Russia. When someone died, he was buried quickly and the bedclothes burned. The red plague, as it was called, was not to be taken lightly. The disease had arrived with passengers on a ship from England, and a dozen had already died in Boston, Papa said, even with a quarantine of the sick.

Mother had no intention of allowing the plague to creep up on us. She got busy mixing chicken droppings, urine from Papa's chamber pot, wood ash, powdered limestone and rainwater to make lye and set us to scrubbing walls and floors to rid the place of the pestilence. For all our sakes, the lye would have to do its work.

MISTRESS PIMMIT

Our new home was set on twenty acres at the north end of Boston. It had nothing to compare with the comforts of our house in England. Although no mansion, the logs of the Charleston house were solid, and never was there such a clean dwelling as when we Lyman women finished our work. Of the two rooms downstairs, one was for cooking, eating and evening prayers, and the other served as a small compartment for Papa and Mother to sleep. John, Richard, Phillis and I shared the upstairs which we partitioned off with quilts hung from roof beams.

The oil paper over the cabin windows let in faint sunlight, but Papa would send to London for glass. In the meantime, we closed the shutters tight against the chill. Although we brought English lamps with us, the oil gave off an unbearable odor. I preferred the outdoors, even in the bitter cold.

My first Boston bed was a sack of homespun cloth stuffed with straw. At night I turned and wiggled, poked and pushed the stiff stalks to find some comfort. Saint Thomas More wrote that a drowning man will clutch at straws to save himself. Precisely how I felt—Papa could grasp the Almighty, but all I had was straw to save me in this foreign land.

At first light, I pulled my shift and petticoat under the covers to warm them with the heat of my body. When I wiggled into my dress, I didn't care about how the wool wrinkled. There were more important matters to worry about.

Even as I shivered, I saw natives snug and warm in their capes of fur and leggings of animal hides. Their skin had a golden flush. The women wore their black hair in braids that fell to their waists. Some of the men had shaved heads that made them seem naked next to Englishmen in their white wigs or locks flowing to their shoulders. The youngsters chewed strips of leathery meat, and women carried cobs of dried corn in baskets strapped to their backs. There was no sign of hardship on their faces, even as snowflakes fell from the sky. They were at home in this strange land. I only hoped I could adapt as well as they.

At dinner one evening Richard said, "We have no meat smoked or grain stored for winter, and the first planting is four months off."

"What did you expect—pineapple groves and trees dripping with fruit and honey?" I asked. "The sea has clams and plenty of fish."

"I'm no fisherman, and Father is a businessman."

"The pork and turnips in this stew came from our neighbors," Papa said, raising his spoon. "We will survive on the kindness and generosity of others until planting season."

"Are we supposed to live like beggars and scavengers?" Richard planted his elbows on the table.

"Maybe we should do like the Indians," I said. "They live quite well."

"I'd rather beg," Richard said.

"Keep an open mind, my son," Papa said. "The natives are Narragansett people, generous with the settlers."

Richard scowled. "My mind is closed when it comes to the unholy barbarians. They're probably cannibals."

"Well," I said, "if you want to feed your stomach, you would do better to open your Puritan heart."

Outside, Ruby nosed the frosted ground in hopes of grass. I pitched her a fork of hay and nuzzled against her steaming side. She was an ox who liked to work and never minded when I fastened on her harness and hooked her to the skid. What stones I could pry loose from the ground I loaded onto the skid for Ruby to haul to John and Richard. They were building a wall to keep the cows from wandering onto the road. Each time John hefted a stone into place, he laid a hex to keep it steady. "Moldy malt worm," he said. When a stone fell over, he delivered more colorful curses. "Pigeon liver," he sputtered. His language was atrocious, but scolding him was useless.

On the afternoon our neighbor Mistress Pimmit hobbled by, clicking the tip of her cane on the cobblestones, she started to pass the wall along our property but paused and watched my brothers work. When we first moved in, Mistress Pimmit had greeted us with a pot of corn chowder carried by a girl who followed behind her. "You can tell she's Pequot by the feathers in her hair," the woman had said. Then she added, "The Pequot are not as hospitable to the English as the

Narragansett, but a gentlewoman needs a servant nonetheless."

I wanted to tell Mistress Pimmit that the Puritan faith required all humans to be treated with kindness and respect. The Indian girl had waited outside in the cold while Mistress Pimmit chatted with Mother. Today she had the servant girl with her again.

"A fine wall 'tis." Mistress Pimmit looked over the rocks at the cows whose warm backs steamed. "I see your father has bought himself a herd." Papa was a wizard with figures and when he charged a fee to keep accounts, some paid him in livestock. The cows were payment as were the dozen chickens pecking at the bare yard.

Mistress Pimmit was plump as a goose and just as haughty. "A stone wall will ne'er do well to keep out the Pequot," she said. "They'll climb over and steal the knickers from your clothesline."

If she understood the mistress, the girl did not let on. She was near my own age and wore a dress with beads and shells scrolling over it in a pretty design. She must have spent hours sewing them on. A beautiful necklace of quahog shells circled her neck. In the marketplace the merchants called the shells wampum and accepted the wampum as money because they could trade it with the natives for corn and beans.

"The natives are welcome to visit us," I said.

"Not this kind, I'll warrant." Mistress Pimmit cocked her head toward the girl. "Help's hard to come by. I've got to keep an eye out or else saucepans vanish and butter dwindles from the churn. Cudgel's the only thing to tame her."

"You see, John," Richard said. "That's the way to handle them."

John blinked. Only in his fantasies had he stood this close to a native in the flesh.

"You cudgel her?" I said.

"Of course."

My stomach rolled at Mistress Pimmit's sickening smile. I didn't even try to hold my tongue.

"Beating servants is contrary to Puritan ways," I declared. "It's unchristian and heartless."

Papa said we must forgive the shortcomings of our neighbors, but I could never forgive that kind of cruelty.

"Well!" The matron pressed her palm against her chest as if acting out a drama. "You'd do the same if you was in my shoes. Bound to be the death of me, she is."

She swung around her snub nose. "You — Pequot! No dallying. Come along." Our neighbor wobbled down the road leaning on her cane, the girl following a few paces behind.

"No wonder she's difficult," I said. "I would be, too, if I'd been beaten."

"The Indian is none of your concern, Sarah," Richard said.

"None of my concern how one human treats another?"

"Not human — savage," Richard said. "How an Englishwoman disciplines her help is her business, not yours."

"But, Richard, it's as good as slavery." In secret, Lizzy and I had read *The Tempest* by Shakespeare, wherein Caliban and Ariel were enslaved by Prospero. And hadn't the Virginia colonies had slaves from Africa for over a decade? Slavery was the greatest evil one person could inflict on another, no matter what my brother said.

Richard set his mouth hard and twisted a stone into place. "Tend to the rocks or we'll never get this wall built."

At Ongar Parrish our hired hands did the farm work and Lizzy and I had been free to climb orchard trees, catch frogs in the stream and eat our fill of wild raspberries. But those days were behind me. I had no time for friends now. With the cattle and chickens to feed, my chores seemed never to end. Until a well was dug, I had to carry bucket after bucket of water from the spring. While Richard chopped, I hauled wood. Inside, I swept floors and fed the fire. Mother and Phillis sewed quilts and bartered with neighbors for kitchen utensils and a few pieces of furniture. In spare moments we made plans to build a corncrib and well sweep, a forge barn and toolshed. With Sunday services and evening Bible readings, it seemed my life was nothing more than work and prayer, prayer and work. I knew enough not to complain, but at supper one night John spoke up.

"Is this barley soup again?"

"Delicious barley soup," said Papa. "I can never get enough of it."

"You're welcome to have mine," John said.

"You need your energy for building the woodshed," Papa said.

"Woodshed? Me?"

"You're just the man for the job."

"Now that barley soup looks more appetizing, does it not?" I said.

John grimaced at me.

"Let us offer the blessing," Papa said. He thanked the Lord for the soup and for our good fortune to have a hearth to warm us and solid ground under our feet.

When Mother raised her head, I saw that the bones of her face pushed hard against the skin. She had been happy in England, but a wife must bow to her husband's wishes. So, dutifully she had packed her most beloved possessions and left the rest to the king's subjects.

I would never be such a worthy spouse. I vowed, too, that I would not let what I owned determine who I am.

Papa noticed Mother's blanched cheeks, too.

"Are you children keeping up with your chores?" he asked.

Richard shot a look at John. "My young brother is practically useless."

"I am not useless, you lumpkin," John said.

"John, mind your mouth," said Phillis, "or I'll have you locked in the stocks."

"Don't frighten the boy," said Papa. "The willow switch will work as well."

John's face puckered. I knew the willow branch was an empty threat — Papa had never raised a hand to any of his children.

"When spring comes, I can drive the plow behind Ruby," I offered.

Richard rolled his eyes. "We want straight furrows, not curlicues."

My elder brother could be so self-righteous. "I handle the ox better than you," I said.

"Please stop arguing," Mother said weakly. I remember watching her tend the gardens at Norton Mandeville—poppies and lilies, primrose and loosestrife, shaking seeds from flowers into a cloth bag she packed into the trunk so her gardens would bloom in America. But there were no gardens here. The ground was frozen. I was afraid my mother's heart was frozen, too.

While I set Ruby to pulling stumps, Phillis took over the cooking to let our mother rest. She learned to work miracles with mussels and clams that John dug from the mud banks. When he brought home buckets of wiggling eels, Phillis boiled hunks of the snakelike fish with parsley and winter savory, roasted or fried them, or stuffed them with nutmeg and cloves and cooked them in broth. So delicious were the dishes that I hardly gave a thought to the fact that I was eating what looked like a serpent. Her baking bread filled the house with a wonderful aroma and made me feel there was at least one warm corner of this dismal town.

Once a week I went with Phillis into Boston for the goods we needed. The village was like a festival. Buyers dickered over prices and street urchins ran among the shoppers. Men strode into church sober and staggered drunk from the tavern in the afternoon. Churches and taverns were the first buildings in town—"One for souls, the other for spirits," I heard someone say. Even Puritans turned to drink when they found the streets in the New World were not paved with gold. The magistrates frowned on drunkenness but kept the taverns open.

From a wooden scaffold in the square, Governor Winthrop laid down new rules for behavior, or Reverend Eliot chided citizens who failed to appear at services. A pillory on the scaffold punished wrongdoers. It seemed every time Phillis and I went to market, we observed someone or other locked in the stocks. The least offense was cause for sentencing—drunkenness, charging too high a price for goods, or even keeping an untidy house.

One afternoon a man grimaced in the contraption. His wrists stuck through two holes, his head in a larger opening. His right eye was swollen shut. At his feet sat a board on which was written "SEDITIOUS WORDS."

"I know that man, Phillis," I said.

"I believe that's Master Chandler," she said.

"Yes, he came across on the *Lyon* with us. But what does 'seditious' mean?"

"Agitating people to treason," she said.

"You mean he spoke out against Governor Winthrop?"

"Apparently, yes. He'll be lucky if they don't cut off his nose."

"The poor man." As in England, Boston's citizens weren't permitted to speak their minds.

"The best way to avoid the stocks is to mind your manners and keep your mouth shut."

I ignored the sideways glance she shot at me.

Phillis bargained for meat and grain while I watched the chattering crowds and frolicking children, the clucking chickens and grunting hogs. Smells from fish monger, spice merchant, and bread maker had me reeling with hunger. All the scents were flavored with the salty aroma of the harbor where ships sat like huge osprey, breathing as the sea breathed.

The Narragansett traded skins and corn for English goods in the marketplace and the colonists shopped next to them. The natives were good farmers. They had planted plots of land just big enough to feed their families.

On one trip, I saw a Narragansett child tug his mother's arm. "*Nip, Okas,*" he said, and the mother gave him water.

"What's he saying?" I asked Phillis.

"I believe he's thirsty."

The boy handed the cup back to his mother. "*Taubotneanawayean,*" she said. The child repeated the word—two-bot-knee-and-away-on—and the mother stroked his head.

"Two-bot-knee-and-away-on," I said. "Thank you?"

"Must be," Phillis said.

Sudden yelling brought my attention to the fabric merchant's table. The merchant was trying to wrench a bolt of cotton from Mistress Pimmit's servant. The native girl clung tight to the cloth until Mistress Pimmit took hold of her braid and swung her around, pitching her into the dirt. The matron then lifted her cane, and the air whistled as the stick came down onto the servant's side. Again she brought the cane down, this time on the native girl's legs. When the girl tried to shield her body with her hands, the merchant pinned her with one knee and slapped her face.

I whisked by Phillis and snatched the cane from the old woman.

"Mind where you lay the lash." I raised the staff above my head. "Or the lash will come back at you."

Mistress Pimmit's face rounded in surprise. "The Indian was stealing," she said.

"If the Pequot wanted to steal," Phillis said, "she would be gone with your cloth before you knew it."

"These people are no better than the wolves," the merchant said.

As if she understood, the girl dropped the bolt into the mud.

"You call yourselves good Puritans?" I threw down the cane and helped the girl to her feet.

Phillis tugged my sleeve. "Come, Sarah. These people have nothing we want."

Lizzy had told me of a game where the English chain a bear to a post and torment it with angry dogs. As the dogs maul the terrified beast to a slow and agonizing death, the crowd cheers. How could the English pray on Sunday and brand a man for what he believes or whip his back into welts? If they could justify beating natives and selling them as slaves to fatten their own purses, who then was more like a wolf?

As for Mistress Pimmit, the cudgel finally came back at her. Two weeks after the incident with the cloth merchant, she came down with the pox and died quickly and mercifully. Neither Phillis nor I shed tears for the matron, and the Pequot girl fled back to her people.

GRACE

"**W**here are you off to, Phillis?" I asked.

My sister was tying on her bonnet. "To a meeting."

"What sort of meeting?"

"Some women are gathering at Mistress Hutchinson's house to discuss—" she stopped and rolled her eyes toward me. "To discuss Reverend Wilson's sermon."

Phillis was not one to tell falsehoods, but I could tell she was hiding something.

"Who is Mistress Hutchinson?"

"She's a midwife," she said. "Her husband is a mercantile merchant, and they have the grandest home in Boston."

"Can't I go with you?" Yardwork had toughened my hands, and sitting in a grand house sounded heavenly even if I had to keep quiet.

Phillis sighed. "You'd be restless."

She was right. I was not eager for more church talk— if that was indeed the purpose of the gathering.

"Tell me what sort of things you thrash out at these meetings."

Phillis took a deep breath before answering. "If you must know, the sermons tell us that salvation comes through good deeds. But Mistress Hutchinson teaches that grace saves us."

I thought about the drunkards and the men who failed to appear in church on Sunday. "What about those in the stocks?"

"Yea." She nodded. "Even those. Every one of us, whether we do good deeds or not."

I had no inkling of what grace felt like but had waited for grace to find me just as I waited for my monthly menses. "Do I not try to do good deeds?"

Phillis straightened my collar and smiled. "Sarah, even you are saved by grace."

It relieved me to know that at least Mistress Hutchinson and my sister believed I was safe from an eternity burning in hellfire.

Phillis attended Mistress Hutchinson's meetings every week except when the weather was too frigid to go out. Still my sister would not allow me to go with her. I suspected the women were plotting something, and I was determined to find out what.

That winter John turned ten without as much as a sweetcake. I'd have given my best petticoat for some of the natives' beehive honey or maple sap syrup to sweeten the bitter cold. My belly rumbled constantly. Papa advised us to be thankful for what we had, but we had so precious little that even gratitude was scarce.

At night our damp boots steamed by the fire. The flames cast more darkness than light on our faces. I tried not to speak of England and Lizzy. They both seemed farther away than ever.

Mother nursed the fire frantically, as much for warmth as to keep at bay the wolves we heard howling nearly every night. As the room grew blue and hazy with wood smoke, I wondered about the natives and how they were passing the evening. I imagined them huddled by their fires telling stories of their ancestors and their hopes and dreams for the future—not unlike us.

When the bay froze over, John gave up fishing. Phillis assigned him to chop kindling, but he groused and was constantly underfoot. He needed a companion.

One afternoon, Papa came home leading a young swine with a fuzzy pink hide.

"A pig is better payment than shillings these days," he said. "He'll grow quickly if we feed him enough. Richard, you'll build a pen sturdy enough to keep him."

"If it means roast pork, I'll build him a palace," Richard said.

"Can I pet him, Papa?" John asked.

"I wouldn't get too close," I said. "He might think you're a bit of roughage."

"Then I'll give him a name, at least."

"Don't get friendly," Papa said. "We may need the hog to keep us alive until next autumn's harvest."

But it was too late—John had already fallen in love with the pig. He called him Sterling for his silvery coat. I'd never seen my brother work so hard. He helped Richard with the pen and raked the sty while the boar gobbled his offerings, what little there were. The natives did not keep pigs. The banks along the bay were studded with clams—delicacies for the natives—but pigs

41

wandering from town tore up the banks with their snouts and hooves and left their stink behind.

John kept Sterling penned to prevent him from damaging the clam banks. The pig was John's friend. When John fixed imaginary golden-tipped arrows on his imaginary bow and aimed at an imaginary white stag that looked very much like Sterling, the pig came and nosed John's knee.

"You're not playing your part, Sterling." John patted the pig between the ears. He spent hours with the pig. In our wretched circumstances, I feared their friendship would come to a tragic end.

January was colder than any I remembered in England. Icy blasts blew down the chimney, and we shivered in front of the hearth. Sap seeping from burning logs hissed and froze even as they blazed. In order to write, I had to warm the ink bottle at the fire. My toes stung as if the embers had singed them. I wished to hibernate like a dormouse until spring.

I thought of the tale of Chaucer's Knight about Palamon, King of Thrace, who rode a chariot of gold pulled by four white bulls. *He hadde a beres skin, col-blak for old.* Palamon could keep his gold chariot if I could have had his old black bearskin that night. Desire was against our Puritan ways, but if I'd had a fur cape like the natives wore, I'd have been as snug as May.

Even through Sunday blizzards we trudged to the church in Roxbury. Bitter wind sliced through my coat and muffler. When I looked toward the sky, I might as well have been underwater, peering up at the frozen surface of a pond. I thought I might drown in the cold.

In the sanctuary we sat in clusters — rich spinsters, young couples with hovering parents, farmers in tight collars surrounded by a throng of children. The building was of stone, and although we sat as near the fireside as we could huddle, the fire did little to warm the room. To baptize a baby, Reverend Eliot had to break up ice in the christening bowl. I brought a blanket to wrap around my shoulders in order to endure the five-hour service. Phillis, however, sat rosy-cheeked without a quiver, her gaze never leaving the face of the minister who issued up heavy prayers and pleas for repentance. Unlike the aging Reverend Wilson, Reverend Eliot was young, handsome, and unmarried. I suspected it was my sister's palpitating heart that kept her warm as she fixed her eyes on him.

When I'd about given up on spring, the sky cleared. Streams rushed frantically over rocks, and icicles hanging from eaves sparkled like slender prisms. Determined violets broke through the frost line and tree limbs grew fat with buds. One Sunday when frost crystals still clung to the windows, Reverend Eliot preached the sermon. Like Mistress Hutchinson, the younger pastor believed grace — not just good works — was the path to salvation, a radical idea for a Boston minister.

"To reach heaven," he said, his voice quavering like lute strings, "cleanse envy and vanity from your soul. Grace will save you from the everlasting torture of God's wrath."

I looked around the congregation. Had everyone received grace but me?

"Oh, sinner," the minister crooned, "prepare for divine justice. The black clouds are even now gathering over your head."

Did one need only to *say* one had achieved grace in order to be saved from Satan's fury? Would it be a sin to proclaim that I felt something I did not feel? Would God know the truth?

"Waste not a moment," the reverend advised. "Grasp now the single vision of hope offered to you this morning." His eyes scanned the congregation, skimming over me and hesitating when he came to Phillis. She sighed, a soft moan of rapture.

I placed my hand over my heart and waited for a sign but none came. Maybe I needed to be a better daughter and sister before I was granted grace. Or perhaps I was doomed. In that case, so were the Narragansett and the Pequot—what did they know about grace?

After the service, I was still contemplating my eternal life when a man approached Papa. He turned his hat nervously in his hands. I could smell aqua mellis on him, which was said to restore thinning hair. His own hair— what there was of it—was as gray as smoke.

"I beg pardon of you, sir—" he said. "My name is William Hills. I have seen you often at church and commend you for instructing your family in the ways of the spirit."

Papa thanked the man and introduced himself.

The man's morally blue eyes rolled toward Phillis. He was at least twice her age.

"Have you family in Boston, Master Hills?" Papa asked.

In Massachusetts, unmarried men were always under suspicion. The constable and a church officer spied on them, reported their actions to the town council, and fined them twenty shillings a week simply for being single. Bachelors could not live by themselves, and families kind enough to offer them a room had to get the town council's consent to take them in. Solitary men were forced either to live with their parents or get married. New England life, hard as it was, made a wife as necessary as a servant.

Good luck had finally come to my sister.

"I intended to have a family, but my dear wife died of consumption last year," Master Hills said. "She never fully recovered from the trip across the Atlantic."

"My condolences," Papa said.

The man ran a finger down his long nose. "I'm wondering, sir, if I might pay your household a visit one evening." Again he looked at Phillis, more bold this time. I may have had no experience in the matters of courtship, but the fellow's intentions were as clear as day.

"Of course," Papa said. "Tomorrow afternoon would be convenient."

Master Hills nodded.

"I'll have my daughter Phillis prepare tea."

"That's very good of you, Master Lyman." Master Hills set his hat on his head, tipped it once as he passed Phillis, and tumbled out the door, barely catching himself.

"Well," said Papa, placing a hand on Phillis's back. "It seems we're going to have company."

On Monday, I swept the house. Phillis rubbed the pewter bright while Mother wiped the table and spread a fresh cloth. I found pretty white snowdrops growing at the forest's edge and picked some for a centerpiece.

"We do want a tidy house," said Mother, frowning at the flowers, "but let's not put on airs."

"It's best if Master Hills sees us as we are," Phillis said.

I smoothed the tablecloth with my palm. Puritan women hardly ever married for love. If they did, my sister would be in the arms of Reverend Eliot. She might desire to be a maiden all her life, but if she chose spinsterhood over marriage, she would be with us for all her days. Not that I begrudged her, but I suspected Papa was eager to have one fewer Lyman mouth to feed.

"Master Hills seems intelligent and courteous." I was making an effort to be encouraging. "The truth is, he's your best prospect in Boston, sister. If you don't marry, you risk being an old maid. Lizzy told me that when a spinster dies, she's condemned to lead apes around hell."

"Don't say hell, Sarah," Mother said.

"I suppose it's better than leading apes around in life." Phillis cast her eyes down. I knew who had her heart and mine ached for her. Maybe nothing would come of Master Hills's courtship.

Mother laid her best linen napkins on the table. "I hardly consider Master Hills ape-like."

"He can't hold a candle to John Eliot." I dared to pronounce what Phillis couldn't bring herself to say. The silence following the minister's name seemed to go on forever.

After a moment Mother said, "Put that thought out of your head, Sarah. Reverend Eliot's work is saving souls. And you're far too young to have designs on the reverend."

"They're not my designs." I turned my eyes toward my sister. Phillis slumped into a chair.

"Heaven help us," Mother muttered.

"Heaven has no part in this." I pulled Phillis to her feet. "Up with you."

Distraction—I needed to distract us both from this gloom.

"Pinch some rosiness into your cheeks. And maybe we can loosen a few tendrils about your face."

Phillis was not lovely, but she was strong and faithful. William Hills would be lucky to have her.

"Tendrils are for young girls," said Phillis, "not for matrons acquiring used goods."

"A husband with experience is much better than one who needs breaking in," Mother said.

"What was Papa like when you married him?" I asked.

Mother unfolded a napkin and folded it again. "He knew very little about women at first, but he was a quick student." She smiled shyly and then tugged her apron straight. "Phillis," she said, "you may find Master Hills a treasure in disguise."

My sister twirled the pomander ball that hung from her sash, sending wisps of dried lavender into the air.

"Tendrils," she said. "I don't suppose the magistrates would fine me for a loose tendril?"

I coaxed a wisp of hair from my sister's cap. "The magistrates will never know."

Phillis made biscuits with flour and lard. I set out a small plate of pickled egg slices. At least our hens were still laying. It was a meager repast for tea but would have to do.

William sat on a wood chair by the hearth, a cup of tea balanced on one knee. I willed his leg not to shake and splatter tea on the floor.

Papa was in a jovial mood. "Master Hills, tell me about your line of work," he said.

Our guest was in the business of thatching roofs, and as he sipped his tea he spoke about buying thatch, applying thatch to houses, and how thatch repels water, keeps in heat in winter and cools the house in summer. He seemed so enamored of thatch that I wondered if the thatch itself wouldn't have made a better companion for him. Yet, my sister had a quiet practicality that complemented Master Hills's passion for his durable roofing material.

While he nibbled a biscuit, Master Hills described his home, which had a cooking kettle on an iron hinge so it could be swung in and out of the fire to adjust the heat. The furniture was fine enough for guests, and he had windows with English glass in them. The thatch on his own roof was of the best quality. Although he wasn't much for gardening, he had enough land for flowers and vegetables and even a few farm animals.

Phillis sat up straighter. She was paying attention, at least. Having so little, she could be forgiven for finding her suitor's property attractive. And by reflection, Master Hills himself became more attractive, too.

There was a pause in conversation. Papa cleared his throat. Master Hills fidgeted. Gratefully, his teacup was empty. I took advantage of the pause.

"How do you feel about the natives, Master Hills?" I would not like to see him mistreat a servant the way Mistress Pimmit had treated the Pequot girl.

"The natives?"

"Yes. Do you believe they receive grace as we do?" Not that I had received grace, mind you, but it seemed important to know his stand on the natives.

"Grace?"

Master Hills was a parrot. Could he discuss anything other than how to keep a dwelling dry?

"Sarah, let's not badger our guest—" Papa started.

"No, no, Master Lyman. Sarah has asked a perfectly appropriate question." Master Hills tugged at his waistcoat as if he were about to deliver a speech. "Trust between the English and Pequot came to a spiteful end after Dutch traders killed the Pequot sagamore who had come to trade with them. The Indians reacted by killing an English trader." He jerked his chin toward the fireplace. "My only interest in the savages is keeping them off my property."

"I see." My place was not to argue with Master Hills, but it seemed to me that killing was not the way to come to peace and trust. Governor Winthrop believed in punishment to maintain civil order, but there must also be a place for penitence and forgiveness as a remedy for bitterness. Could they not all declare the score even and begin anew—in friendship? Master Hills, the good Puritan man, would not agree. Were I a Pequot native, I'd surely stay clear of his property.

Two weeks later at Saturday evening supper, Papa announced that Master Hills had asked for my sister's hand in marriage and he had given his consent. Phillis was no goddess, but Papa had built a successful business. He was intelligent and had such an air of dignity that the magistrates had appointed him to be an official in the General Court. The Lyman name, even in so short a time, commanded considerable respect. Master Hills no doubt considered an alliance with our family a propitious prospect. Phillis was fortunate. She would always have a roof over her head — albeit a thatched one.

The wedding ceremony would take place in the spring. Finally, I had a ray of light to brighten these last bitter weeks of winter.

TWO WOLVES

In the dead of night I heard all manner of noises. Mice scratched in the kitchen and an owl cried a mournful hoo-hoooo. Farther off, there was the doleful wail of a wolf, the most lonesome sound I'd ever heard. Other nights the wolves held a party—hollering in harmony, talking over each other, a call and response. The howls sounded almost human.

The next morning Richard said, "We lost another chicken last night."

"Was it a fox?" Papa asked.

"There's no sign of struggle," Richard said. "Most likely it was an Indian. They have a taste for fowl."

"It could very well have been a wolf," I said.

"The Indians bay to make us think they're wolves, and then they sneak close to our pens." Richard planted fists on hips.

"I didn't hear chickens cackling," I said.

"The savages wring their necks," Richard said.

"Why would you think it was natives who took our chicken?" It annoyed me that my brother laid every misdeed on the natives. They were more accustomed to this land than we and looked to be well fed without stealing one of our scrawny hens.

"It is spoken in the village that the Pequot are thieves."

"It was a wolf," I said, "or a fox. Not a Pequot."

"Don't be naïve, Sarah. One day you'll wake up in an Indian camp and find savages have carried you off. Maybe they'll throw you in the cauldron and make a soup out of you."

"Richard, you are infuriating!"

"Daughter," Papa broke in, "it is against the Puritan way for a lady to argue."

"But Papa—"

"Hold your tongue, girl."

Papa was siding with Richard. But even worse, he was talking like the rest of the colony. I had assumed in Massachusetts Papa would think for himself. He disappointed me.

Master Hills dined with us twice a week. He always brought a hunk of ham—which John refused to eat on account of Sterling—or a pound of mutton for the stew pot. When he arrived with a bundle in his arms, he was a welcomed guest.

At supper, Richard brought up the topic of our missing chickens.

"I wouldn't put it past the Indians to take your fowl," Master Hills said, "but if it is indeed wolves after your chickens, our homes won't be safe until we're rid of them."

"There's a bounty on wolf hides," Richard said. "Fifteen shillings each. I wouldn't mind getting a reward for bringing in a hellhound skin over my shoulder."

I bit my lip and stood to clear the plates. I tried—honestly I did—but I knew I could not keep my silence for long.

"Wolves were here before people," I said. "The natives don't kill wolves. They are like brothers."

"Brothers?" Richard said. "Brothers don't take your chickens without paying for them."

"The English have killed off most of the deer," I said. "Wolves come after our livestock to keep from starving." I wasn't protecting the natives—I just wanted to avoid the killing of any beast—or any human.

"Maybe it's not wolves or Indians," John said. "Maybe it's werewolves. I read about them. They look just like you during the day." He glared at Master Hills, who had made no effort to win John's favor. "At night they grow fur and fangs. They'll kill every one of us if they get the chance."

Master Hills sniffed. "Load of poppycock."

"Hush, John," Phillis scolded. "You're just trying to frighten us."

I stifled a giggle. I had to agree with Master Hills regarding werewolves. Poppycock indeed.

Then Mother spoke. "I heard them, too. It wasn't natives and it certainly wasn't mythical creatures. I believe Sarah's right—it may have been wolves."

I got up from the table and kissed her on the cheek. I didn't need to say anything—the silence spoke loudly enough.

One afternoon while pitching hay to Ruby, I sensed eyes boring into my back. Two travelers were on the road, faces turned to each other in conversation. Richard and

John were at work repairing the wellspring behind the house. Then I looked across the meadow. Standing on the ridge was what looked like a large shaggy dog. But not a dog—more like a bear. Even from so great a distance I caught the flinty odor of wolf fur.

Thick shag of coat—gray, brown, black flecked with white as if snow had fallen on her back, her head. White belly. Yellow slanted eyes. Nose a black plum. Mouth friendly, laughing. Wolves travel in packs to hunt, but this creature was alone. She meant me no harm.

I don't know how long we stared at each other, neither of us moving, each of us curious about the other. When prey runs, predator pursues—I knew that much. I stood my ground and hoped the animal couldn't hear my knees knocking together. Slowly, she turned and started toward a thicket of brush. Before she disappeared, she took one quick glance back at me.

"Farewell, sister," I said.

The next morning I woke to John's wailing. Fumbling into my dress, I hurried downstairs. Richard and John were outside in Sterling's pen. The two stared at the ground where a pool of dark blood had soaked into the dirt, spots of red trailing toward the swamp.

John wiped his nose with the sleeve of his shirt. He didn't want me to see he was crying.

"I hate to say it," Richard said, "but you were right, Sarah. Natives wouldn't leave such a mess. Whatever took the pig had a struggle. Natives would have carried it off, but it looks like Sterling put up quite a fight."

I wished we could live peacefully with the wolves, but our settlement was in their territory. We were the invaders. They were just trying to stay alive.

"We could build a barn to hold the animals at night," I suggested.

"Even if we could find the wood, that would take a month." Richard paced across the pen and back again, shielding his eyes with a hand. Peering across the field, he said, "Wolves are like ghosts. They move too fast to shoot. I'll get some men to help dig a pit outside of town and cover it with brush. It's the only way we can trap the scoundrels."

"And if you catch one?"

Richard didn't answer. He didn't need to.

While Richard was gone, John and I did his chores. Afterward, Mother and Phyllis cooked supper and I read my lessons. If Papa had found Chaucer's book, he had not scolded me. Anyway, I kept it hidden under my bed to read by flickering candlelight.

At dusk, Richard appeared, his clothes caked with dirt, his cheek smeared with clay.

"Where did you dig?" I asked.

"Sentrie Field by the river," he said. "Benjamin has seen wolves wandering there."

"How deep?"

"Deep as Benjamin is tall. We tied ropes to buckets, and he filled them until he was in a hole high as the top of his head."

Benjamin Davenport had become Richard's first friend in the village. He was of the same age and a decent sort.

"We had to haul Ben out with a rope," Richard said. "No wolf will leap out of that pit."

"You'll capture maybe one wolf," I said. "What good will that do? You'll wear yourself out digging holes."

Richard sighed. "I'm too tired to argue with you tonight, Sarah. Let's just wait and see what happens."

A loud bawling awakened me in the night. I sat up in bed and listened. Two animals, I thought. Two wolves? Was one of them the wolf I had seen on the rise?

Finding my feet on the rough floorboards, I stumbled for my dress and boots. Outside, a half-moon hung in the western sky. It was well past midnight.

Richard came out with his musket. In the doorway Papa grimaced and rubbed his hip. He must have had an ache, which had caused him to limp.

"Stay, Father," Richard said. "It's probably nothing."

"I'll thank you for that," Papa said.

"I'll come," I said.

"No, you won't." Richard pointed a finger at me. "You'd be wolf meat. I'll get Ben out of bed."

When Papa went back inside, I crept to the woodshed and felt my way toward the corner. Ruby's gamy scent reached me along with the promising aroma of tender shoots in the spring-fed meadow. Without wind, dew on the field crystallized into frost and I shivered.

Rather than risk being seen at the gate, I climbed the fence. When I jumped over, my skirt caught on a post and ripped the cloth. I'd have to explain to Mother or mend the tear before she noticed.

Across the way, I caught sight of two men hurrying toward Sentrie Field, one carrying a torch and the other a musket. I followed Ben and my brother at a distance, sweating now even in the cold.

Something felt very wrong.

As I neared the pit, I saw Ben holding up the torch. He was staring into the crater.

"Looks like we caught two scavengers," he said. "Maybe we should let them be—they'll do each other in and save us a musket ball."

"Are they wolves?" I said.

"Sarah!" Richard yelled. "Get back! I told you—"

Richard tried to grab me but I twisted out of his reach. In the pit's shadows I saw that fur covered only one creature. Without doubt, the other was a man.

The wolf turned in circles, its wiry fur brushing the man's legs—but its teeth were not bared. It was not even threatening to attack the man.

"It's an Indian," Ben said. "Why in the name of all that's holy aren't they trying to kill each other?"

The man looked up at us. "*Mogkeyóaas*," it sounded like he said.

"What does he mean?" Richard said.

"*Mogkeyóaas*," the man said again. "Great spirit." He pointed at the wolf.

The native spoke some English. How much did he understand, I wondered?

"Bah," Ben said. "Great spirit that robs our dinner."

"A wolf and an Indian are one and the same," Richard said. "I ought to shoot them both."

Ben laughed. He thought Richard was joking, but I knew my brother better. Richard was right about one thing, at least. The wolf, the native, and the settlers of Boston — all were the same in my eyes. Is that what grace meant — compassion for all things?

"Let them go," I said.

The laughter stopped. Richard glared at me as if I were a stranger.

"I said let them go." My voice had fire in it.

Someone had left the rope coiled by the pit. I tied one end around a stump. The loose end I dropped into the cavity. Richard and Ben watched but neither said a word.

The native walked himself up the side of the pit and stepped out. He was taller than Richard and not much older than I — a teenager. He wore a type of leather vest. His hair was loose and streamed past his shoulders, shining in the torchlight. Around his right arm was a band of some sort. Braided rope? No — the design was part of his skin. A tattoo of intertwined strands.

He stared at the three faces that peered back at him. When he saw me, the brave cocked his head. I think he knew I was the one who rescued him. If only I could speak to him, to apologize for my brother digging the pit. But I didn't have the words.

Richard lifted his musket. I held my breath.

"Be gone!" he called, shaking the musket.

The brave turned and looked down at pit. The animal leaped, its front paws scratching at the earth to get a hold. Then it fell backward and yelped. The brave kneeled and reached toward the wolf, but the beast pressed itself against the wall.

Then the brave stood and lifted his arms toward Richard as if holding a musket of his own.

"*No bushkwa*," he said and shook his head.

"Richard, he's telling you not to shoot," I said.

"How do you know what the savage is saying?" Richard called again. "Be gone, I say!"

The brave took one last look toward the wolf and then vanished into the darkness like a puff of smoke.

I reminded myself to breathe. In the pit, the wolf's eyes glared yellow.

"Kill the fiend before he makes a meal of your ox," Ben said.

Richard aimed his musket at the wolf. I reached for his arm, but he jerked away and pulled the trigger. The hammer clicked and the gun exploded. The musket ball tore into the animal's side. I heard a scream and the wolf fell limp.

To this day, I don't know whether the scream was the wolf's cry or my own.

SEEDS OF DISCONTENT

Reverend Eliot preached that we should banish sinful thoughts from our minds, but I struggled to banish them from my stomach. Even with my best efforts, I could not help but envy Master Hills for visiting the tavern every evening after supper. A pint of ale was filling, and he could learn the latest gossip from the other patrons. Some of that gossip reached the Lyman front door.

One morning as I was sweeping the kitchen, a distinguished-looking man appeared at our threshold. He was tall with a pointed chin.

He pulled off his hat. "My name is Thomas Hooker. I've come to speak with Richard Lyman the senior, if I may."

I asked him in and called Papa.

"An honor, Reverend Hooker," Papa said, shaking his hand.

I took the reverend's cape and hat and hung them on a hook. Papa offered Thomas Hooker a seat in the wooden rocker. As he rocked, Reverend Hooker explained that he had recently come from England and had conferred with Governor Winthrop here in Boston.

"What news is there?" Papa asked.

"Many of the townspeople have complained about the governor's laws," Reverend Hooker said. "Some citizens are calling for a public election to unseat the magistrates Winthrop appointed."

I sat listening and fiddling with needlework. Although I knew it was rude to eavesdrop, between Mistress Hutchinson's meetings and Thomas Hooker's visit, I sensed some change was afoot and I did not want to be taken by surprise.

"Are we not better off than under the rule of King Charles?" Papa asked.

"Half the Puritans left England because of the king's public whippings. Some Puritans got worse—noses slit and cheeks branded." He tugged at his belt. "Leaving England was the last resort for many who could no longer tolerate having their freedoms taken from them."

"Freedom is one thing," Papa said. "Putting food on our plates is another. Here in Boston even those with money cannot find a bushel of corn to buy."

"The stew is coming to a boil," Reverend Hooker said.

I had heard talk in the marketplace. Everyone seemed to be in a sour mood. Boston was not turning out to be the promised land that Papa dreamed of back at Ongar Parrish. But did they have to talk about stew when we were hungry?

Reverend Hooker rocked back in his chair. "When I pressed Winthrop about his appointments of magistrates, he threatened to send me back to England," he said. "No man in Boston ought to have that much power."

The reverend was at least a decade younger than Papa and looked to be more fit. There was a spark in his eye, and I believed he meant to shake up the colony. It was about time someone did.

"Do you have a plan?" Papa asked.

"Yes," the reverend said, "and I want to know if you and your family are with me."

What was the plan, I wondered? The elders were plotting my future. Should I have nothing to say about it? There wasn't much about Boston that pleased me, but on second thought, if Reverend Hooker's plan involved plenty of victuals, I might climb aboard.

A few days later, Papa gathered us to the table. He said a blessing over our paltry meal. Then he began.

"I believe Reverend Hooker has the right idea," he said. "We came to Massachusetts as equals, and we should have an equal say in how we are governed."

Richard was staring at my bracelet. I had traded embroidery in the marketplace for clay beads and threaded them onto twine. What was the harm in a simple bracelet?

"You'd best get rid of that adornment or you'll be put to the lash in the public square," Richard said.

Mother had embroidered the edges of the very tablecloth where we were sitting as well as the hem of my dress. Wasn't embroidery adornment? The natives were not lashed for beads that embellished their dresses, their quahog necklaces, or the feathers in their hair. Shouldn't we have the freedom to honor our own handiwork?

"I'm tired of the rules here," I said.

My family was used to my outbursts by now, and even Papa had given up admonishing me.

"No one chides the natives for the way they dress," I said. "I should be permitted to wear a halter and bridle if I desire to. If conditions don't improve, I shall suffocate."

"Sarah—" Papa's voice was gentle. "We cannot risk any behavior that draws attention." He stroked his chin. "But how would you like it if we lived in a place where you could speak your mind and don your beads as you wish?"

"I could wear whatever I liked?"

"Within reason." Papa sat up straighter. "Reverend Hooker has spoken of the wide meadows of the Connecticut Valley with fertile soil and sun like honey."

"Where is Connecticut?" I asked.

"To the west," said Richard. "If we leave soon, we can spend the summer building homes and planting before winter."

"And how do we know Connecticut will be any better than here?" I asked.

"We have details to work out, of course." Papa looked around the table at his family. "Are you game?"

"I am," said Richard. He had taken over managing the farm, and I was surprised that he was so ready to uproot.

Mother chased a bean around her plate with her spoon.

"Wife?" Papa said.

Silver strands glazed her hair, and lines drew from her eyes like dry creek beds. My mother was the only daughter of a Leeds schoolteacher who slapped learning into his young students. She was just fifteen when she married Papa, and I wondered if she fell in love with him because he offered her escape from her father.

"You are not a young man, husband," she said. "Oughtn't we leave Connecticut for those with more —" She hesitated. "Vitality?"

Papa dipped his head and peered over his spectacles. "I give you my word that I shall muster as much vitality as a man with fewer years under his doublet."

Mother collected the dishes from the table. "Of course," she said. My mother was a dutiful Puritan wife who would never dispute her husband's ideas. She modeled proper behavior for Phillis, but I was — what was the word? Intractable? Stormy, I think it meant. Unmanageable. The word suited me. If we were given minds to think and language to express ourselves, why shouldn't we honor those gifts?

"We must make our decision soon," Papa said. "Governor Winthrop or Connecticut."

That my parents might get old had never occurred to me. Papa was frailer than he had been in England, but he had given his promise to do what was best for his family. I only hoped his decision would be what was best for me.

Phillis looked lovely in her simple dress. I had festooned my own dress with ribbons and pestered our mother until she allowed me to sew a line of lace at the neck. The magistrates did not allow such decoration, but no magistrates would be attending the wedding, which was to be held in our great room. My sister had fashioned slashed sleeves, which were the style in England, and she stitched a bodice from a piece of silk I found in Mother's chest. Lace and silk and slashed sleeves were all strictly forbidden which, to me, made the dress all the more beautiful. In my hair I pinned downy feathers hanging from my curls like fledgling birds and swore Phillis to secrecy until just before the ceremony when our mother would be too concerned with wedding details to pay my dress any mind.

Papa glared at my outfit but held his anger until the guests had left.

"You could have me called to the General Court for your behavior," he said. Papa's endurance was wearing thin. "The magistrates will question my control over such a wayward daughter."

"The Puritans have no sense of fashion, Papa."

"Fashion has not concerned your mother, your brothers nor I," he said.

I looked at his shoes. "You could do with a spur buckle on your boot." Papa was still wearing shoes from the 1620s with a rosette on the toe. I was wrong to challenge him, but I stood my ground.

"You are not to mind my footwear," he said. "If the constable hauls you into court, you'll have to plead your case yourself."

I threw back my shoulders. "Don't worry — I will. And I'll do it in my most colorful finery."

After Phillis moved into Master Hill's thatched house, I wasted no time in taking over her space, but I hadn't expected that Mother would order me to assume her household duties, too. Cooking did not come easy for me, and I got used to sliced knuckles and singed fingers. My first meal of roast chicken was near disaster. The poor, headless bird was so underdone it all but squawked. The potatoes were mealy and the bread so heavy it would have served well as a doorstop. Mother proclaimed me more fit to scrub pots, for which I was much relieved.

I dreamed of a succulent roasted goose and plum pudding, but food was in such short supply that I was dwindling away to nothing. My shift hung on me like a sack, and I cinched my apron tight around my waist. Every month more ships arrived in Massachusetts Bay, and thousands of new settlers spread into surrounding towns. When supply ships docked, people fought over bags of grain and spools of wool. There was not enough timber for building new houses, and the woods were laid bare for firewood. Newcomers set up tents for themselves or crowded in with kindhearted citizens. Livestock grazed in the few open meadows that should have been planted, and cows and oxen suffered for want of hay. We were fortunate for the natives who traded their corn for English goods. Otherwise, half of us would have starved.

Papa, too, was losing faith. Although he said nothing, he and neighbors gathered from time to time by the corncrib or at the stone wall between our properties and talked in low voices, their eyes scanning up and down the road for anyone who might overhear.

While I washed dishes, I complained to Mother. "Governor Winthrop has given us the freedom to attend services but not the freedom to think. I'm tired of having to watch every tiny thing I say or do."

"Are you finished with those pots?" Mother dried the dishes and stacked them on the shelf.

"Yes, but—" I was just getting warmed up. I wished my mother were better at conversation.

"Listen to me, Sarah." She anchored a hand on each of my shoulders. "Governor Winthrop threatens to banish Anne Hutchinson for having meetings with town goodwives."

"For what? They're just discussing Sunday sermons."

"Not just sermons. The governor says Mistress Hutchinson is organizing a rebellion against the leaders of the colony."

"That's nonsense. Phillis has attended those meetings. She would have told me of a rebellion. Will they banish her, too?"

Mother wiped her hands on her apron. "Master Hills has forbidden Phillis to go to further meetings."

"Why shouldn't Phillis be allowed to go wherever she chooses?" I pouted. "She is a wife, not a servant."

"If Mistress Hutchinson is banished, where will she go, Sarah? She has fifteen children." Mother's voice trembled. "What will those children do if their mother is driven out?"

"Would the magistrates really banish a mother and her children?" I asked.

She squeezed my shoulders. "Indeed," she said. "Is it not better to keep still and do as you're told?"

I broke free from her grip.

"No," I said. "No, it is not better."

Mother ran her hand over the smooth tabletop. After a moment, she said, "Daughter, you are fifteen years now. If you continue to dress and speak as you do, you will be put into the stocks. That is, if you are fortunate. If you are not...." She stopped, drew a deep breath, and stared into my eyes. "Some magistrates might accuse you of practicing witchcraft. You could be in grave danger."

I had read about what happened to women convicted of being witches. In England Queen Mary had ordered hundreds burned at the stake for heresy. They were tied to a post with kindling strewn about their feet. Fire caught the hem of their dresses and burned blisters on their legs. Yet still they lived until their skin was charred black and their hair seared to the scalp.

But that would never happen in America — at least, not yet.

"You can't frighten me into obedience, Mother," I said.

"I only tell you the truth. And, Sarah, I will be unable to help you. No cries to heaven will help you."

The hot licks of fire were a torture beyond imagining.

"In that case," I said, "I have but one word."

"Yes, child?"

I lifted my chin. "Connecticut."

THE SECOND FAREWELL

There is nothing fair about farewell.

In June 1635, we had lived in Boston for nearly three years. Three years was long enough to bear the constant threat of punishment for the simple act of speaking our minds.

Once we had packed our furniture and home goods for the journey to Connecticut, the ceiling beams of our Charlestown house looked grand in the bare room. The tall hearth was as cold as my heart, but a ray of morning sun blazed through the eastern windows and cast rectangles of light on the wood floor. With any luck, the sun would shine as bright in the valley of Connecticut.

"You'll be sure the midwife is here when the time comes, won't you, Master Hills?" Mother looked at my sister's swollen belly.

"My wife will have the best care money can buy," he said. "You have my word."

"I haven't given up hope that you'll join us in Connecticut," Papa said.

"Perhaps next year," Master Hills said. "Your houses will need sturdy roofs."

I knew he was not intent on moving. His thatching business was profitable, and he and Phillis were starting a family. With so many arriving each month and in need of housing, Massachusetts would keep him busy and wealthy. Anyway, Phillis was in no condition for a long foot journey. Next year, no doubt she would be with child again, another excuse to stay in Boston. Phillis said her husband believed if he minded his own business and abided by Governor Winthrop's laws, they could live well and have a passel of children. I didn't agree, but I had no say in the matter.

As a goodbye gift, Master Hills gave John a new hatchet. "It will serve in helping build the settlement," he said. To Richard he presented a long knife for cutting our way through the wilderness. Phillis gave Mother a tablecloth with the letter L embroidered at one corner — for Lyman. The material was not fine English linen, but Mother was pleased and traced the letter with her fingertips. I was thankful she did not weep. Leaving was difficult enough.

Phillis handed me a bundle tied with ribbon — a scarf with matching mittens.

"For Connecticut's winters," she said. The winter would be devilishly cold without my sister's warm body to press my feet against or her warm hands to rub the red chill from them, but I would feel the comfort of her fingers in the knitting of the scarf.

I pulled a string of purplish quahog shells from my skirt pocket and draped it around her neck. She blushed and pulled her wide collar over them.

"Our secret," I said.

She put her hand on the collar. "Our secret," she repeated.

I swallowed the sob in my throat. "One hundred sixty kilometers, that's all it is from here to Hartford," I choked out. "It's like from London to Coventry. That's not so far, is it?"

My sister knew me before I had a voice. When I started to speak, I sassed her so many times that I would not have been surprised if she wished again for those days before I could talk. She had been by my side for all of my fifteen years. How would I live without her?

Phillis cupped my cheeks and brought her face inches from mine. Mother said a woman carrying a male child has a rosy complexion, but Phillis was pale — the sign she would have a daughter. A girl to replace me.

My eyes felt hot, and my sister's face blurred.

"You have important work now, Sarah," she said. "Care for Father and Mother. It's your duty now. Mine is here."

I forgot about Puritan manners and wrapped my arms around her, our stomachs pressing against each other. When the baby moved in her belly, I gasped.

Phillis laughed into my ear. "She seems to know you."

I bit my cheek and held onto my sister. I knew the hazards. Our mother had lost three baby sons, and it was a miracle any woman survived childbirth at all. I pulled away and studied her face. Phillis was six years older than I, and in a decade I would look like her, maybe even with a protruding belly of my own. Whether facing the wilderness or the magistrates, I knew that life was unpredictable. I knew, too, the possibility existed that I'd never see Phillis again. It was a thought too hard to bear, and I welcomed her familiar wisdom.

"I can read your thoughts, sister," she said. "Let's not dwell on the future but live only in this moment and the next."

For her sake—and the baby's—I tried my best to be happy for her. Being happy for myself was another matter.

THOMAS HOOKER'S EXPEDITION

Thomas Hooker's group gathered in Newton, west of Boston on the Charles River. A hundred travelers scurried about, yoking oxen to skidders, tying on tools and instruments for carving a town in the wilderness. There were a few horses, but most that survived the voyage from England were lame or too weak to travel far. I still wished we had kept our workhorse Lofty, but our trustworthy Ruby would have to do.

The plodding trek to our new home would be our second long journey, though not so long as the voyage aboard the *Lyon*. Each time we loaded our trunks, we left more behind. The Indians had fewer possessions than we did, and being unburdened by so many chattels gave me a sense of freedom. Except, of course, Chaucer's book of tales — I would never leave Lizzy's book behind.

It would take a fortnight of traipsing with such a crowd of laden but determined souls. Richard stole glimpses at Patience Taylor, the strawberry-haired beauty whose family joined our party. He might have tried to speak to her along the way, but Benjamin Davenport and their friend Christian Hector called him up ahead to help clear the trail with his long knife. I followed close behind, ripe for an adventure.

"Keep an eye out for panthers," Christian said loud enough for me to hear. He was a year older than Richard.

"Mountain lions?" I said.

"Precisely. Black bear forage these woods, too."

If he was trying to scare me, it wouldn't work. I was not going to show fear, no matter what.

"Panthers and bears won't come after so many of us," I said.

"I'm not worried about us. You'd be hardly more appetizing than a toothpick," Christian said. "They'll go after the livestock."

The livestock were a serious consideration. We had herded five dozen cows along the trail, a slow effort, stopping in grassy fields to allow them to graze and at streams to water them. In desperate times, a cow would bring a fair price that would keep our family in provisions. We could not afford for a cow to be dragged off by a predator.

"If we come upon a she-bear with cubs," Benjamin chimed in, "a mother bear will attack in the flutter of an eye."

"A bear might take a young calf but can hardly handle a full-grown bovine," I said. "A she-bear will scoot her cubs up the nearest tree. She won't bother with us."

Benjamin and Christian were witty and stout-hearted, and they were baiting me with stories much like the ones Chaucer's characters invented on their pilgrimage.

Benjamin pressed his sleeve to his forehead and mopped beads of sweat. "She'll have to find plenty to eat if she's to nurse twins. And she has a strong sense of smell. A pig or some chickens would do her nicely."

I knew he was right, but I wasn't about to give in.

"Bears eat bugs and berries," I said.

"When they come out of hibernation, anything in their way is fodder."

"Then I suggest you lead the way, Ben." I was joking, of course. Nevertheless, I kept a wary eye on rotting logs and fallen trees where the furry creatures might be digging for dinner.

Richard patted the stock of his musket. He had practiced until he could shoot a piece of broken crockery off a log at a hundred paces. When I asked if I could have a try, he said, "Ha! You could barely lift this flintlock, much less load and fire. Even then you'd be lucky to hit the side of a woodshed."

My brother could be exasperating.

We had strapped a crate of brood hens to Ruby's sled balanced with some seed corn, potatoes and soldier beans, and we prodded forward our herd of sixty cattle.

Natives had broken a path, but the way was so narrow that families marched single file through the forest, driving the cows ahead of us.

After hours of hiking, Richard pulled a compass from his vest pocket, turned it in his hand and squinted into the afternoon sun.

"We should be heading southwest," he said.

"Toward that mountain?" asked Christian.

"That's the direction, yes."

"Can't we go around it?" I asked. "We'd have to use the prod to get Ruby to pull the load uphill."

"Ruby's strong enough," Richard said. "And the underbrush will be thinner as we go higher."

And so we began the climb, cattle and travelers ranging in age from infants to Papa, the eldest among us. Most of the men had lived prosperous lives in England and weren't used to such physical effort. Yet shod in hobnail boots, every man carried utensils and weapons on his back and whatever else he could handle along a trail barely a meter wide.

My own pack was heavy, but I didn't mind. Chaucer's book and the quill, ink and paper inside the pack were like wings the air lifted. I had to remember the details of this pilgrimage to our new home, every musky smell, every sturdy pine and oak reaching toward heaven like the pillars of a cathedral, their tops a green dome. I forced myself to remember the moss growing soft on outcroppings and streams that played over rocks like babbling children. Someday I would tell Phillis and her youngsters of this journey so they would know what we had done.

The only feet to tread this path before us wore moccasins and left no imprint. I would have liked a pair of moccasins to ease the corns on my toes from the English leather, but everyone suffered equally. Women carried their share of the burden, too. Thomas Hooker's wife was buxom, and on the third day of travel her toe caught a tree root and she fell and bruised her hip so badly she couldn't walk. John Lyman reported this unfortunate event with much out-of-breath embellishment.

"Mistress Hooker's gone lame," he panted. "She fell and tore her dress and got dirt all over her. Reverend Hooker sent me to fetch the boys. You, too, Sarah."

We followed John back to meet the group of hikers. The reverend's wife stood on one foot, balancing awkwardly.

"Richard," Papa said, "you, Ben, and Christian will have to assist Mistress Hooker if we're to make it to a campsite tonight."

The three exchanged looks, but no one made a move.

"Quickly now," Papa said.

"After you, Richard," Christian said.

Patience Taylor gazed at Richard like an adoring fawn. "So gallant of you," she said, strands of sparking hair falling from her cap.

Richard seemed to puff up with strength. He reached for Benjamin's arm, glancing at the redheaded beauty.

"Ben, we'll make a seat. Christian can spell us in half a mile." He glanced at Patience to be sure she was watching.

Benjamin and Richard linked elbows. Christian took the matron by the waist and lifted her onto the boys' shoulders. She wobbled at first, and Richard steadied her with his free hand. Perspiration seeped through her bodice, and she emitted an aroma of some exotic flower. The moldy scent of rotting leaves would have been more pleasant. With one arm firmly around each boy's neck, the convoy resumed its way up the mountain slope. I picked up Richard's musket, slung it over my shoulder, and marched behind. If I had a chance to fire the rifle, I'd show him I could hit more than a woodshed.

At the crest of the ridge, we stopped for water and the men lowered Mistress Hooker, relieving them of their burden. Richard rubbed his shoulder. Below, the valley rolled out like a velvet carpet. Surely we were in Connecticut by now. The air smelled of warm stones, and sun gleamed on the hardwoods so that they looked like torches lighting the way. I didn't want to miss the twitter of a single bird, the twisting of a solitary leaf on its stem.

"By God's grace," Papa puffed, "I'd gladly suffer the *Lyon's* slanting decks again rather than heave myself up mountains." He limped to a boulder and leaned against it.

"Rest a minute, Papa," I said. His face was flushed and damp with perspiration.

"Had I known we would tromp through mire and jungle to be whipped by branches and pricked by thorns, I'd have given Connecticut a second thought."

Blood had seeped through his wet sock.

"Let me see your foot." I unbuckled his shoe and saw a blister on his heel had broken open. It would become infected if not tended to. Papa would do better to walk barefoot until the blister healed, but that was out of the question.

Mother had made an ointment from dried marigold blossoms, and I dabbed some on the blister then packed leaves in the heel of the shoe.

"This will raise your foot so the blister doesn't rub against the shoe," I said. "That will help."

We had crossed swollen streams on fallen logs, cut through thickets and traversed swamps, but I hadn't realized how difficult the trail might be for Papa. I should have stayed near him, but wasn't I helping to move the group in the right direction?

Papa took off his hat and dabbed his brow with a handkerchief. "Have I prayed and labored and dreamed for nothing?"

I tried to raise his spirits. "We can camp in the clearing below. Tomorrow you'll feel brighter."

He pressed the handkerchief back into his pocket. Tomorrow we had another twenty kilometers to cover, and I suspected the terrain would be no more hospitable than today's. Richard would not be strong enough to carry Papa, not even with Benjamin's help. Papa would have to keep up his courage a while longer.

Richard and Benjamin made a litter out of saplings for Mistress Hooker and strapped it to a horse. Dragging her saved their shoulders even if it was a bumpy ride for the mistress.

As we started down the other slope of the mountain, Richard took the musket from me. I kept alert for the rustle of a bush, a flash of movement. If I flushed out a fat partridge and Richard's aim was true, we'd have a feast for the dinner pot. We'd had no meat the last two nights, and I had lost my taste for corn mush.

Up ahead, Christian stopped and peered into the trees. If he had heard an animal, I knew not to move or even to blink until he took aim. A good-sized deer would feed the entire company with nothing left for the scavengers but bones.

Slowly enough so as not to disturb a mote of dust, Richard raised his musket. If the breeze blew our scent toward the animal, he didn't have a chance of getting off a shot before the game dashed away. Pressing his cheek against the stock, he squinted one eye and sighted down the barrel. He was aiming too high for a rabbit, and if he were after wild turkey, the gun would move to follow the bird's strut. But he was standing still as ice. I wished he'd pull the trigger and get done with it, and I braced my knees for the explosion of gunpowder. He'd have one good chance to kill the animal. By the time he loaded the musket again, the creature would have taken flight over logs and be lost in the woods.

Why was he taking so long? My mouth was salivating for turkey or hare cooked on a spit.

When my curiosity reached its limit, I turned in the direction the barrel pointed. Through saplings straight as flagpoles, I saw brown legs. Yes, deer! We could feed twenty hungry wayfarers that night. Wait—not four, but six legs.

I blinked.

These legs belonged to no deer.

I looked for deerskin leggings, beaded belts and the quahog necklaces of the Narragansett. This time of year they would have moved from their winter long houses back to the shores of Massachusetts. They were good hunters and friendly with the settlers. If these were some of the Narragansett stragglers, they might share their game with us. But the braves in front of us wore only loincloths decorated with designs. One young brave fixed his eyes on mine. His hair fell down his back. Hair of straw color. White lines of paint ran from his forehead to the tip of his nose. Around his neck he wore a necklace of red-tail hawk feathers, and on his arm was a band of rope drawn on the skin. A tattoo.

An image flashed across my mind of a brave and a gray wolf.

"Pequot," Benjamin breathed.

Through the woods I spotted two more natives and doubtless there were others hidden in the trees. The braves stood so still they looked to be carved from oak. Even though they stared down the barrel of Richard's gun, there was no sign of fear on their faces. I touched the beads at my wrist and remembered the feathers in my hair. I was wearing a dress, not the paltry piece of deer hide Pequot women wore, but the natives must have thought me strange. Who was this curly-haired English girl adorned with nature's ornaments?

The young brave with the hawk feathers still peered at me. How odd that the other natives had shaved heads or hair of shiny black, so dark it was almost blue. I knew if the brave had the courage to face a wolf in a pit, he had no fright of a white boy with a gun.

What was the word — the word he had said in the pit? Mog-key-something. Why could I not remember it? It meant great spirit. If the power protected us as it protected these Indians, we would pass each other in peace.

Suddenly, by some precious miracle, the word came to me.

"*Mogkeyóaas*," I nodded at him. The brave nodded back.

"Lower the gun," I said.

Richard seemed deaf.

I grabbed the rifle barrel and pushed it down. "I said lower...the...gun."

The din of cattle lumbering through the brush reached us, and I turned to gauge how close they were. When I looked again into the forest, the natives had evaporated into air, but I could feel the eyes of the tattooed one, hot as pellets against my skin.

VANISHING CATTLE

In the clearing we broke into family units, rolled out our pallets and built fires to cook simple meals. We milked cows and dipped our mugs into milk buckets. After we had eaten, I went with Richard to check the livestock. The last few nights we had left the cows loose to graze during the night. They were tame and wouldn't wander away.

"Here," Richard said, handing me a coil of rope. "Help me tie them together. We'll stake them to trees in clumps of five."

I didn't ask why he wanted to tether them tonight — I had a feeling the Pequot had something to do with it.

When we had secured the cattle, Richard said, "You go back to camp. I'll stay with the livestock."

"I'll stay with you."

"It's all right. I'll wake and check on them during the night."

I was glad not to win this argument with my brother. The day's hiking had worn me out and all I wanted was to crawl into my bedroll.

Settling down, I looked up at the only lodging nature offered — the jewel-studded sky. Wind swept the treetops. An owl hooted a hollow, mournful call, and a tree limb cracked. For Papa's sake, I hoped Connecticut would be as Reverend Hooker had described it, a place of beauty where citizens could govern themselves freely. When Papa was Richard's age, he was building his own homestead in England. He was middle-aged when he married, and by the time his first child was born, he was thirty-two. It seemed that all his adventures had come late in life. Now he had a chance to live his dream of a plantation even more splendid than Norton Mandeville, a home nestled in a valley surrounded by rich pastures.

Dreams of meadows and bountiful harvests pushed thoughts of bears, mountain lions, and wolves from my mind. As for the Pequot, they must have tucked themselves into their own bedrolls by now. I listened to the cattle nosing the ground and convinced myself that Richard and the cows were safe. Then, without so much as a sigh, I fell into an exhausted slumber.

During the night I woke shivering. The fire had died to embers and the campsite was pitch black. I couldn't hear a sound — not the heavy breathing of John's sleeping nor the sigh of a breeze or snort of a cow.

I rolled to my stomach and pushed myself to my knees. How had it gotten so cold? Wrapped in my blanket, I got to my feet, careful not to make noise that would wake the others. I had to find Richard and make sure he and the cattle were just as I'd left them.

It was so dark — were my eyes open or closed? I stumbled forward, hands feeling the blackness ahead of me, hoping to grasp a horn, a tail. But I couldn't even smell the cattle, their sweet, pungent odor. What if panthers had killed them—would I trip over their carcasses or would the panthers have dragged them off? No, I would have heard them bellow. And where was Richard?

My family were just steps away, but in night's shadow I might as well have been completely alone. I wished I had nudged John awake to come with me. Benjamin and Christian were sleeping with their clans, and there was no chance of finding them in the darkness. The cattle had to be fine. Hadn't Richard and I roped them just paces away in a grove of trees?

When I caught the scent of pine needles, I knew I was nearing the place where we had anchored the cows. I touched a tree trunk and felt sticky sap on my fingers. The ropes must have come loose, but I was sure the animals would stay in the area.

"Richard?" I murmured. "Richard, are you here?"

"Aye," he answered, his voice full of sleep.

"What have you done with the livestock?"

"They're right here, where we tied them."

I heard him scrabble to his feet and was glad to feel his warmth.

"Smart cows to untie our knots then," I said.

He felt the tree trunk and the ground below it.

"The ropes are gone, too." I could hear panic rising in his voice. "Ruttish wagtails!" He slapped the tree trunk. "What sort of fool-born clots would steal from us?"

"Wait until first light." I was trying to stay calm. Losing our entire herd could mean our ruin. The cows were our milk, our cheese, our meat, our very prosperity.

"If we don't find them, we'll search. They're docile and won't have gone far."

Then he was almost pleading. "You're better with animals than I am, Sarah. You gave them names — call them."

I accepted the rare compliment and cupped my hands around my mouth.

"Bluebell! Scarlet! Buttercup!"

No sound came back.

"Daisy! Nutmeg!" Not even pleasant-scented names made their dung smell any sweeter. But nary a leaf was disturbed.

"I'm sure we left them right in this grove." Richard sounded crestfallen. He pressed his back against the tree bark and lowered himself to the ground.

"Maybe we've gone the wrong direction," I said. "They're probably right under our noses."

I squatted next to Richard and leaned my head against the trunk. Cold or not, neither of us would move until daylight shined upon a herd of Lyman cattle.

When morning dawned, I squinted up at Richard standing with arms folded across his chest. Around him were piles of drying dung, the ground tamped down by heavy animals. There was no other sign of the beasts.

I scanned the woods. One of Reverend Hooker's hired men was tending his cows, and the blankets were mussed where he had slept among the herd. I should have stayed with Richard instead of lying by the fire, but hindsight did us no good now.

For half an hour we roamed the nearby woods looking for signs of the cattle.

Nothing.

When we returned to the grove where we had tied them, I said, "We'll have to tell Papa."

Richard dropped his arms and brushed leaves and dirt from his britches, but he made no move toward the Lyman campsite.

"Why would the animals wander off when they've never done so before?" I asked.

"Someone led them away. Someone who can steal up on animals without a sound. Someone who seized a fitting opportunity."

Richard leaned over and picked up a feather at his feet.

"It was the Pequot," he said.

"How do you know?"

"How else would the cattle disappear?"

By my brother's ineptitude, I started to say. But I held my tongue. This was no time to toss kindling on the embers.

Richard broke a twig and tossed it into the woods. "What do we say to Father?"

The trip had tried Papa's spirit. He had hardly spoken even to Mother. A gremlin melancholy had a grip on his heart.

"Losing the cattle could kill him," I said.

"Damn the Pequot," Richard said.

"If the Pequot stole our cows, it is because we are in Pequot territory."

Richard didn't debate me, but he worked his mouth as he was building a defense for himself.

"Where do you see fences?" he said. "Or stone walls to mark their territory? And where are their deeds to these lands?"

"The natives don't need fences and deeds," I said. "They believe the land belongs to everyone."

"But not the cows — they belong to us."

"They left us Ruby and we should be grateful we still have the ox."

My brother offered his hand and pulled me to my feet.

"Without a herd of clumsy heifers," I said, "we'll be as light-footed as the Pequot. Let's find some joy in that."

"I am not rejoicing that we'll have no milk or beef to start us out in Connecticut," he said.

As he stroked the quills of the red feather, I realized without a doubt that we would not see the Lyman cows again.

THE CONNECTICUT VALLEY

Because of the wide river that flowed from the far north to the ocean on the southern coast, Reverend Hooker had given our new territory the name Connecticut after the Algonquin word *Quinetucket*, meaning "beside the long river." Our new town he named Hartford, the place where harts — deer — forded the river.

Over the coming weeks, I would come to know the river. Boston's Massachusetts Bay was saltwater, but here the river carried fresh water, excellent for irrigating farmlands. Deep and wide, the river offered us sturgeon and freshwater mussels which, if we competed with otters for them, had not the sweet taste of the mussels we dug from the mud banks in Boston but filled us nonetheless. Falcons and white-faced eagles built nests along the shore, and if I hadn't had fieldwork, I could have spent an afternoon watching them dive for fish.

Years before we arrived, Dutch traders built roads and a fort to protect against Indian attacks, Reverend Hooker told our group. He said to beware of the Pequot, a warring tribe that claimed much of the territory we aimed to settle. Papa said we were on a divine mission and the Lord would protect us. He had better be right.

We set to work clearing and spent the summer planting and building houses to make a village. I had thought Connecticut would give me respite from hard work, but what did I have to show other than strong arms and callused hands? Although money was not worth much in our new settlement, Papa purchased two cows and a bull from another colonist. If the cows had calves, we would have milk and butter and could start to build a herd. In the meantime, we each depended on the others to lend muscle. Richard and John learned building skills, and neighbors grateful for help with their own houses paid them in eggs and cheese.

Our house occupied the south side of Buckingham Street, the fifth parcel of land from Main Street. Through two glass windows, dawn blazed out of the east in the early mornings. The glass was full of ripples and bubbles, and in the evenings I tilted my head and watched the moon change shape as if it were alive. The slightest breeze made the trees wiggle.

The meadows and woods surrounding Hartford were as untouched as they must have been when Adam and Eve were cast from the Garden of Eden. Winter brought snows that made the hillsides glitter. John and I slid on smooth boards down the slope with such peals of laughter that were we in Massachusetts Bay might have sent us to the stocks. At other times John fooled me with his pranks. Once, when he watched me making fritters, he asked if he could help. I let him fry a few. When I turned my back, he dipped wads of cotton in the batter and fried them, then put them on a plate.

"Here, Sarah," he said. "I made you a surprise."

Suspecting nothing, I complimented him on his thoughtfulness and took a bite of his nasty gift. At least Mother reproached him for wasting batter.

On cold evenings the Lyman family gathered around the hearth, giving me a sense of peace that made me believe nothing could be amiss in the world. In the warmth of the fire, I wondered about Lizzy and how she was spending her time. I supposed I was no longer English, but what was I becoming? I was beginning to feel like a stranger even to myself. The Miller's Tale spoke of emotions. *Lo, which a greet thing is affeccioun! Men may dyen of imaginacioun.* Die by imagination? No one knows for certain how Chaucer died except that his death occurred in the year 1400. Maybe his imagination did him in. In that case, I resolved to stop dreaming and harness my emotions—my affections, as Chaucer said. Instead, I would live each moment with gratitude and rein in my galloping thoughts. If I failed, I might suffer the fatal consequence of the Miller's Tale.

The ink for my quill dried up, and I used a stone to crush butternut shells. I boiled the shells in water and added vinegar and salt to set the color. For black ink, I sprinkled in lamp soot and made myself a new quill from a crow feather sharpened with a knife.

When the fire died out in the night, I nestled deeper under the quilts until daylight when I heard Richard drop wood onto the embers and get the flames stirring again. Once I was dressed and moving about, I didn't mind the cold so much. Somehow Connecticut was not so frigid as Massachusetts where a bitter wind came from across the bay.

When the New Year came, ice closed up the river like a lid over an eye. Between winter and spring, the ground was still too hard to plow but the sun heated the top of my head as I sat on a stump and watched the village bustling with life, the scarf Phyllis gave me wrapped about my neck. Hammering from barn building and the clunking of axes splitting wood became familiar sounds. In the evenings, families gathered in groups to share meals.

Within months, Hartford had become scarred with muddy trails and pastures marred by the hooves of livestock. There was no stopping civilization. Reverend Hooker supervised as men erected a church, our first community building. I woke and slept to the sawing of logs and chopping of hatchets as a town grew up where before were only deer paths.

As spring arrived, every unfurling leaf caught my attention. I listened to the squeak of two limbs rubbing together and learned the difference between the tender call of a crow to its mate and the caw-caw-caw of danger. I heard the hawk's wing slice the air, the tiny scratching of a mouse's foot, the grunt of groundhog, the press of deer hoof against pine needle. Wind whistled through the forest and water mumbled under the edge of river ice.

With warm weather, natives appeared on the outskirts of town. They set up their camps a short way from the village, and on quiet evenings the sound of their drums carried to Buckingham Street. Some nights there was an eerie animal-like howling that belonged to no wolf I'd ever heard.

"What is that sound?" I asked Richard.

"Some of the natives have caught the smallpox." He paused in his wood splitting and leaned upon his axe. "Those drums are funerals for the dead. Don't go near that camp, Sarah."

During the smallpox outbreak in Massachusetts, we learned the symptoms—fever, sweating, red blisters all over the skin. The Pequot lived so close within their teepees that smallpox spread like a forest fire. When someone died, he and all he had touched were burned in a cremation pyre. The smell was so rank that I took to carrying a handkerchief to hold over my nose when the wind blew toward Hartford.

"The natives must have caught the pox from the English." I stacked the split wood against a tree. "Maybe Mistress Pimmit's Pequot girl brought it to her village."

"We survived the plague." Richard swung the axe at a log. "It must be divine justice that the disease is clearing the Indians from our township."

"There's nothing divine or just about the plague," I said.

"Who are we to argue with Providence?" Richard rubbed a shoulder. "Besides, they're encroaching."

"En-what?"

"The Pequot move their cook fires nearer our village every day. What do they want with us?"

"We're fortunate they tolerate us," I said. "No doubt they camped here for fishing long before we settled."

"Do you know what Pequot means, Sarah?"

"It must have something to do with water," I said.

"The Dutch gave them the name. It means 'destroyer.' I've seen them by our wall at nightfall, and in the first light of morning they're outside the wall still. They're watching us, and they mean us ill." He tossed a stick of wood toward me.

"They keep a distance. What are you afraid of?"

"I'm not afraid," Richard growled, "but they are a warring people. And they don't understand English ways."

"Do you understand theirs?" I asked, but my brother went back to his chopping without giving an answer.

MINNO

Our house was not far from the church. Because the place of worship was built in the middle of town, it was named Centre Church. To attend Sunday meetings, we crossed a newly-built wood bridge over Little River that ran south into the Great River. I had come so far after crossing the ocean on the ship *Lyon* that finally I could delight at water rushing under my feet, especially with land just a few steps away.

Reverend Hooker was not only the minister but also Hartford's governor. Although he preached about their ungodly ways, Reverend Hooker let the Pequot be. I was curious about them, though, and despite Richard's warning, I spied on them from behind rocks and trees. Wrapped in skins, women worked outside the wigwams, their faces painted with as much elegance as the wealthiest dames of England—red and black on their cheeks and red in the center parts of their dark hair. With babies wrapped to their backs, they split wood into strips and soaked them until they were just the right softness to weave a basket or a mat to sit upon and cook. They molded clay into pots, decorated them with shells, dried them in the sun, and buried them in embers until they were hard enough to set on the coals.

The Pequot children were ocher-skinned beauties. One girl came to the edge of our pasture to watch Richard lay well stones. She wore a hide strapped about her waist as a sort of skirt with a pouch dangling from it. I was writing in my journal, and the curious girl peered over my shoulder. She giggled at the lines on the page. I handed her the quill and pressed her fingers to the stem, showing her how to dip the quill's tip. She drew circles on the page and giggled again.

I took back the quill and drew a curvy line.

"S," I said. "Sarah. That's my name."

"S," the native child said. "Say-rah."

"You?" I pointed toward the girl.

"Minno," she said and wiggled her hand like a fish. She was a few years behind me in age, I reckoned, although it was hard to tell with the Pequot. Even the grandmothers looked years younger than my own mother.

"Minno — little fish?"

She smiled. I laughed.

I drew straight up and down lines and handed the quill to the girl.

"Now you," I said. While she copied the letter, I considered that I might make a good teacher. Was such a thought vanity? If so, I was yet another step away from receiving grace. Maybe I was not cut out to be a Puritan at all.

The child put down the quill and touched my cheek.

"*Netop*," she said. "Friend."

"You know English?"

She nodded. "Traders teach me."

"Dutch fur traders?"

"Yes. Beaver. Fox. Rabbit."

"Wonderful!" I said. Finally — someone to talk to.

"Come," she said.

I followed her to a spring where she picked ferns, their fronds curled tight as fiddleheads. She held out two handfuls.

"Cook. Eat," she said. "Good." She patted her belly.

That night I cooked the fiddleheads and added salted pork.

"Where did you get these greens?" Richard asked. "They're delicious."

"They grow by a spring," I said. It was no lie. And Richard was right — they were absolutely delectable.

A few days later, Minno appeared again, carrying a bucket of sweet-smelling water.

"What is this?" I asked.

She pointed to a maple tree. "From tree. Boil. It is good."

That evening I did boil the sap on the stove, although I wasn't expecting much. Shortly the steam filled the house and made my mouth water. In an hour I had a syrupy liquid. I dipped cornbread into it and delighted in a sweetness like nothing I had ever tasted.

Another time Minno brought me a basket of nuts.

"Paukauns," she said and dumped the smooth shells into my apron.

I took the nuts to Mother.

"These are pecans," she said. "The most delicious of nuts. Wherever did you find them?"

"Secret trees," I said.

She took a wooden mallet from the shelf. "Help me crack them. We'll make a nut pie."

It was a delicious pie we flavored with the maple syrup. After that, Mother asked no more questions about my gifts of food. No doubt she believed I was learning to forage by myself.

Minno met me nearly every day except Sunday, which was reserved for church services, supper, and visiting. I nodded off during the slow hymns, but walking home through the meadow, the music wafting from the Pequot camps gave me a sense of joy. I thought of the centuries of natives who had lived in harmony with the wilderness, and their pounding drums brought me more alive than I had ever felt.

One day when Minno arrived at my tree stump, she brought a band woven with thin strips of hemp, wooden beads and pieces of bone. She pulled off my bonnet and tied the band around my head so that the hemp crossed my forehead. Then she stood back and grinned.

I unwrapped my sister's knitted scarf from my shoulders and wound it around her. It seemed a fair trade, one beautiful handmade thing for another. I didn't think Phillis would mind.

Later that day while I did my chores, I wore the headband instead of my cap.

"Sarah," Mother said, "take that vile thing off."

"I don't see anything vile about it. I think it's handsome. We came to Hartford to do things in a new way, did we not?" I didn't mean to offend her, but I had started down this road and I would walk it to the end.

"We came as Puritans, not as Indians," she said.

I wiped a spill from the tabletop. "I will not wear it into town."

"You will not wear the horrid object at all," she said.

"But it was a gift," I said. "From Minno."

"Minno?"

"A girl."

"An Indian?"

"Yes," I answered truthfully and in defiance added, "Pequot."

Mother yanked the band from my head, pulling my hair. "You will not go near that child," she said. "Her people carry diseases." Whirling around, she threw the hemp and beads into the fire.

I often act before I think, and I stuck my hand into the fire and grabbed the band from a burning log. The cuff of my sleeve caught and my hand stung from the flames. The beads were smoking, and I beat my arm against my skirt to stop the burning.

"You've singed your cuff," Mother said. The damage to the precious English cloth was more important to her than my burns.

"You had no right," I said, sticking my hand into the water bucket.

She opened her mouth to speak but instead turned to the sock she was mending. Without looking up, she said, "Put some ointment on your burn and then go help your brother bring in the kindling."

That evening Papa forbade me to talk to Minno again. Obviously Mother had told him of my insolence. He was sitting on the edge of his bed and looked sunken in his rumpled winter robe, nightcap pulled over his skull.

Wanting to sound like an adult, I used the formal address of a daughter to her father. I thought that would make a stronger impression on him. "My lord father, all God's children share the common air together."

"The Pequot are not God's children," he said.

"Then whose?"

Papa raised his index finger in the way that signaled he was about to announce something important. "Mr. Hooker and the other town leaders know far more than you about the Pequot. The Indians are dangerous, daughter."

"But Minno is just a little girl."

"She is a savage." He stood and looked down at me. "And you will do as I say."

"Yes, m'lord." I couldn't help it if the "yes" sounded like a hiss. At least for that night I let the matter rest.

I reasoned that seeing Minno one more time would only be proper courtesy. When she came into our meadow in the afternoon, she had my scarf tied under her chin and the same basket over her arm. I thought she might have more pecans to give me, but in the basket were white clouds. She offered them to me and I munched a handful.

"What is it?" I asked.

"Corn." She worked her mouth until she found the word—"popped."

"Popped corn? Who taught you how to make this?"

"*Okas.*"

When I frowned, she said, "Mother."

"Ah—*Okas*. And how do you say father?" I had heard the word from a child in Boston.

"*Osh*—father. *Ohke*—earth."

The words were so much alike I'd have trouble remembering which was what.

"How do you say God?" I asked. Surely the Pequot believed in God.

Now it was she who frowned.

"I mean the big spirit." I pointed to the sky.

"No God," she said. "*Michabo.*"

"What is *Michabo*?"

"Great White Rabbit."

"Your god is a rabbit?"

"Great White Rabbit," she said again.

It made sense that the Indians would believe in a creature of their own world rather than a spirit they couldn't see. If the Greek's Zeus could be a swan or an ox, why shouldn't God be a rabbit?"

Minno motioned for me to follow her into the woods. I was getting used to these adventures and wondered what she had in store for me this time.

I looked back at the house and saw that Richard was helping a neighbor build a shed. Papa was at the town hall on some business. He had plans to build a bigger home, a frame house with a wood floor. I might have my own room with a door that closed — a small room, but big enough.

How did Minno sleep in her wigwam? On a mat of woven reeds laid out on the ground? One small space for her whole family? At a certain age a girl needs privacy. My own monthly flux had begun, a pain Mother said I would have to anticipate. I wondered — how did women of Minno's tribe deal with such a nuisance? Minno had no fat to her, and her skin was as brown as if she had fallen asleep in the sun. When she ran, her bare feet made no sound and the ends of the scarf swung and flapped against her bare chest like long, floppy ears.

Sunlight shined through a break in the trees and danced on the early ferns, washing the green to a pale yellow. Along the path, Minno stopped and held up her hand, signaling me to halt, too. Into the waist of her skirt she had stuck a knife with a bone handle. At her other side was a length of braided hemp. Slowly, so that she barely seemed to move, Minno pulled the hemp from her belt. One end had a loop and the other end a knot. She stuck two fingers into the loop and held the other end in the same hand. Then she picked up a smooth stone and set it in a pocket at the center. She swung the strap around her head and at just the right moment released the knotted end.

Like a glint of light against silver, the rock flung toward a mass of brown fur. The fur leaped and twisted, feet clawing at wet leaves to get a grip before it fell limp.

Minno ran to the animal and lifted it by the scruff of its neck. Then the knife appeared in her hand. I came closer to watch. She cut a slot in the coat and began skinning the mink as if undressing a doll. As she peeled the skin from the mink's stomach, I saw a leg twitch. She had only stunned it.

"No, Minno!" What I meant was, kill the animal. Slit its throat. Don't let it suffer. But she held the little creature down, its legs now tearing the air to get away, and continued to sever the membranes holding skin to muscle, her face showing no emotion.

I found a heavy rock and kneeled by the mink's head. Saying a quick prayer to the animal's spirit, I brought the rock down quickly, smashing its skull.

Minno freed the fur from the last tendons holding it to muscle and stood, presenting the pelt to me. The fur, still damp with life, hung lifeless and bloody in her hand.

Was it so easy to kill? My own people killed animals in order to live. How was the mink any different from a chicken or a hog? And how could I ever explain a mink skin to my mother?

Instead, I took the hemp rope from Minno.

"What do you call this?" I asked.

"Sling," she said.

"Sling," I repeated. "Teach me to use it."

HATCHETS AND TOMAHAWKS

Minno showed me how to make my own sling. We braided strings of hemp twice as long as my arm and in the middle twisted braids for a pocket that would hold a rock. We made a loop at one end and tied off the other end.

Then she showed me how to throw. She slipped the loop over my middle finger and had me hold the other end in my fist. Then she settled a smooth rock into the nest. Standing a short distance away, she motioned for me to raise my arm and swing the hemp in a circular motion. When the sling picked up speed, I let go of the loose end to send the rock flying. At least, that was the idea. On my first try, the rock fell out of the pocket and knocked me on the head. The second time, the rock tumbled at my feet. By the third try, I got the stone to fly a short way. With practice, I thought I might acquire some skill with this rock slinging.

"David used a sling like this to slay Goliath," I told Minno. When she scowled, I realized she would have no way to know who David was, much less Goliath. Was there even a Pequot word for "giant"? I gave up — there was no point in trying to explain.

Every morning I practiced throwing with my sling. I perched a gourd on a rock and aimed at it. After fifty tries at ten paces, I hit the gourd. Then I backed up to twenty paces. A dozen more tries and finally I knocked the gourd off the wall. The sling, I concluded, was better than a musket. It took minutes to load a gun and two hands to shoot it, but a sling was ready in seconds — the time it took to pick up a stone.

I discovered that smaller rocks traveled faster and farther than larger ones. Smooth rocks flew straighter than jagged ones. At the stream, I gathered stones polished by water and piled them next to the woodshed — my ammunition. It took long hours of practice to hit a moving target, but over the next few weeks I brought home squirrels and once a fat wild turkey. Even Richard was impressed.

John was more interested in his hatchet than in my sling. He sharpened the blade with a whetstone and felled small trees, chopping them into firewood. I'd never seen such industry from my younger brother. Tall and leggy, he was nearly thirteen now. Connecticut was agreeing with him.

One morning while I was cutting dry squash vines in the field, I saw John take aim at a broad maple. He readied the hatchet behind his ear and let it fly. The blade struck the tree and clunked to the dirt. He slurred an oath, retrieved the hatchet, and walked back to his throwing spot. Taking a hop forward, he flung the hatchet again. It spun once and bounced off the tree into a bed of ferns.

"Villainy," John cursed, pushing away the fronds. He was outgrowing his more colorful swears.

Across the clearing, a native in soft leather chaps watched. His skin was golden, not like the pasty color of my brothers. John still had his boyish softness, but this man was as smooth as marble. His straw-colored hair fell straight down his back, and he glowed with health.

The native moved closer, two dozen paces behind John. I recognized the necklace of red hawk feathers. Around his arm was a tattoo, a braided rope—the man in the wolf pit. The young brave in the woods on the path to Connecticut.

In his fist he held a tomahawk. Slowly he raised the weapon and pointed it toward John.

My breath caught. Why would the Pequot throw his tomahawk at my brother? What had John done to aggravate him?

I grabbed my sling. Goliath wore armor that covered all but his forehead. David must have practiced his skill with the sling or had exceptional luck because with one single river stone he struck the Philistine smack in the center of his forehead. To hit the brave I would need all the luck I could muster. I searched for a rock, but I had cleared the garden and there was nothing but clumps of dirt.

I yelled "Whoa! Stop!" but the tomahawk was flying forward. The blade sailed past John's nose and dug sharply into the tree.

John froze.

I froze.

The brave could have split John's skull, but he had aimed at the tree and hit the trunk square. When I found my breath again, I had to admire the fellow's skill. If John had leaned a centimeter forward, the blade would have struck him. Maybe the brave was giving John a warning but whatever his intention, I was going to defend my brother. I found a stone in a garden furrow and kept my sling close at hand. If called for, I knew how to use it.

The brave glanced at me. I wondered if he remembered me. The pit. The trek to Hartford. I hoped he meant us no mischief.

The native marched to the maple trunk and plucked loose his weapon. The tomahawk looked to be part of his hand. Tied to the handle with rawhide, the blade glinted in the daylight. He found John's hatchet in the ferns, handed it to him and marched again to the throwing spot. John hesitated and then followed. Standing next to him, the brave hefted his tomahawk over his shoulder and waited. Even from the garden I caught his scent. He smelled like water. Like rocks and sand and reeds. Like the forest itself.

John imitated the brave's motion, lifting the hatchet as he did. The man reached for John's elbow and raised it until the elbow pointed toward the maple. Then he swung his own tomahawk forward but didn't release it, demonstrating how to flick the wrist. Finally, he threw the tomahawk and the blade bit the trunk square and true.

"*Wiskenoo*," the native said. Then he looked at me and nodded toward John. "Young brave."

I was surprised to hear that he spoke a little English. Dutch traders again, I guessed. But with hatchets and tomahawks flying through the air, I was anything but at ease.

Across the garden, Minno was watching and I wished she would tell the brave John and I were no threat to him. But Minno's calm face taught me calmness.

John found his balance, raised his elbow, pursed his lips and threw, snapping his wrist the way the Pequot had shown him. The hatchet buried itself in the trunk just below the tomahawk. The Indian nodded once, almost a bow. Then he pulled both tomahawk and hatchet from the tree. He handed John his tool.

"*Wunne,*" he said. "Good."

The brave turned toward me again and stared until I lowered my gaze. Being self-conscious was a new sense for me. When I raised my eyes, I saw that he was smiling, his teeth white as summer clouds. Then he stepped toward me. I stood straight, refusing to back away. Whether it was nerve or idiocy, I would not show fear.

He was so close to me now that I could have reached out and touched his chest. It was hard to gauge his age, but he was younger than I had thought—eighteen, I would guess. In his eyes I saw innocence and goodness. I knew he intended me no harm.

He wedged the tomahawk into a pouch at his waist and slowly drew a necklace over his head. I hadn't noticed it under the feathered necklace. This one was more beautiful with a string of clay beads with one purple abalone shell in the center. As he pulled it off, the necklace fanned out his long hair and I caught a whiff of oil of some kind. A clean scent.

Taking the necklace in both hands, hands that looked too delicate for a warrior, he stepped closer so that I could feel his breath on my face. My heart thumped in my chest, but I made myself trust.

The beads passed my forehead, my ears, my hair, and rested heavily on my neck, the abalone shell against my bodice.

Then his hand was on my arm. I shivered. The palm was so hot that a shock went through my body almost as if lightning had struck me. I gasped.

The brave stared into my eyes, and I was gripped by a strangely familiar sense. I had known this boy, this man, before — before the pit. Even before we came to Massachusetts Bay. It was impossible. And yet I was never so certain of anything.

When he wheeled around and tore away, I searched for the words to call him back but I was struck dumb and could only watch his heels kicking up high behind him.

Had I dreamed him? My hand went to the necklace. No dream. There it was, the abalone shell still warm from his own skin. Why were my knees shaking? And what was this strange new feeling that gripped me?

It was not until the Pequot disappeared into the forest that I looked for John. He was still at the tree, his jaw slack as he stared after the brave.

Minno waved and came to the garden.

"Who is that man?" I asked.

"*Kizzen*," she said. "Brother."

"The brave is your brother?"

"Yes," Minno said. "No."

"What do you mean, yes — no?"

"Same mother. Not same father."

Minno must have seen my confusion.

"His father — he is Dutch. Trader of fur."

I began to understand. That's why the brave looked different from his fellow tribesmen. He was half

European but lived among the natives rather than follow his father to Holland.

"He has seen you." Minno seemed to be searching for the words.

"In Hartford?"

"No. Before."

"In Boston." I said. "With the wolf." It was not a question.

Minno nodded again.

"What is his name?" If he was going to keep popping up out of nowhere, I thought I ought to call him by name.

"Ayaks."

"Ayaks," I repeated. "Does it mean something?"

She pointed to the sky. "Star."

Star — a gigantic sphere of energy that looks tiny in the heavens. His mother must have seen a glow of light in her infant. But a star keeps its distance. Come too close and a star's brilliance blinds and burns. And yet — how many have yearned to know a star's mysteries?

So I would call him Ayaks, not Star. Ayaks was a name that felt foreign on my tongue. I wished I could ask Minno the meaning of the necklace. If only she could speak better English. Then again, we were in Pequot terrain and I should have been learning her language.

RUNNING WOLF

The Pequot possessed more talents than throwing tomahawks. I watched them build their wigwams, driving saplings into the ground, lashing them to one another with rawhide and hemp. They covered the frames with bark and woven cattail mats and hung a flap of deer hide over the doorway. Smoke from cook fires plumed through an opening at the top. The wigwams had no windows, but the Indians spent little time inside except to sleep. Nothing unnecessary. A good way to live.

While I sat on the riverbank with John, our fishing lines dangling in the water, the Indians paddled out in canoes. For months I had watched them carve the boats out of tree trunks. Others waded into streams and set out weirs woven with branches and brush to catch half a dozen fish at once. They dipped out shad with baskets or brought up squirming flounder and pickerel on the tips of their spears. John watched and at night worked on weaving his own net from twine. When it was finished, he took the net to the river and cast it out as he had seen the natives do. From then on, our skillet was never empty of fish. Living alongside the Pequot had definite benefits.

One afternoon a group of natives gathered on the nearby field and tossed around a ball of wound skin which they caught in small baskets attached to the ends of sticks — a game of some sort. By swinging the stick, one threw the ball from the basket to a teammate and ran down the field to catch the next pass.

Richard watched from the front porch, scowling.

"I should scare them off with gunshot," he said.

Papa shook his head. "We've taken in the harvest. Let them have their play."

John stepped off the porch and ventured close to the field. Whooping and yipping, one team worked their way down the field toward a goal — a broad tree. Players from the other side intercepted passes or knocked the ball from a basket to claim the prize.

I had never seen such running. They dashed nimble-footed, stick baskets in hand. Ayaks led the charge up the field. His body had formed the muscles of a man, and sweat glistened on his skin. Watching him gave me a pleasure I could not restrain. When his pitch hit the goal, he whelped, "*oodle-oodle-oodle*" and waved his stick in victory.

The next time he had the ball, a player knocked into him and I saw the man's ankle turn. The native got up hopping on one foot. Play stopped. Ayaks caught sight of John on the sidelines. He took the injured player's stick and held it out to my brother.

John stood dumbfounded. Ayaks took John's hands and squeezed them onto the shaft. Then he motioned John into the game. As John jogged onto the field, Ayaks threw a quick squint at me. My heart felt as if it had flipped over, and I pressed my hand against the abalone shell to slow the swift beating.

Mother had stared at the necklace with such wrath that I was convinced she wanted to set it afire, but she made no move to take it away. She must have suspected that the necklace had more importance to me than Minno's headband.

John took the stick and sprang down the field. No one passed him the ball but from the smile on his face, it seemed he was enjoying himself. When he got near the goal, John whooped and looked for Ayaks. Just as Ayaks hurtled the sphere, John lifted the stick and the ball found the basket. He took three long strides and hurled the prize toward the tree. When it clunked against the trunk, the players crowded toward him. They hefted him aloft and carried him down the field.

Finally they set him down, and the limping brave clapped a hand on John's shoulder and said some words I didn't understand. Then, "You run like a wolf," he said. "We will call you Qaqi Muks — Running Wolf."

Near dark I was out in the garden digging up carrots when I spied Ayaks at the wood's edge. He studied me and then lifted his hand and waved me to follow. I looked around and when I was sure no one was watching, I entered the forest behind him.

Sun dappled the moss on the trees and peepers squealed in the lowland. He led me up a rise where the ground was dry then stopped and turned toward me. Grabbing my wrist, he drew me down next to him onto a soft bed of pine needles. He held my arm tight, even when I twisted my hand to release it. At first I was frightened, but then another feeling gripped me, one for which I had no words.

I ran my hand over his bare chest, cool and smooth as glass, and felt the rise and fall of his breathing. He untied my bonnet, his fingers soft on my cheek. His lips, too, soft on my neck. I might have pushed him away, but some force overpowered my will. Strength left me and I melted into the forest floor, his warmth next to me.

It seemed as if only minutes had passed before darkness settled around us. Had we fallen asleep? I pulled myself away from Ayaks, an act that took all my power. Maybe we were wrong to be alone together, a native boy and an English girl, but I felt no shame. Ayaks ran his fingers over my collarbone, over the necklace, whispering words I could not understand but that I knew meant he felt the same. I struggled to my feet. How I longed to stay with him until the morning sun cast its golden eye upon us! But Mother would be worried and Papa angry, and I wished not to be the cause of their alarm.

From the windows of the Lyman house a candle burned. Inside, Mother had left a plate of supper for me, but I passed it by and went to my room. No food would satisfy this hunger.

At Sunday meeting, Reverend Hooker declared, "The Pequot Indians are idle and lazy."

"As idle as a foraging bear," John murmured.

Our mother gave him a silencing glare. But John was right. And, anyway, what was wrong with moments — even hours — of idleness? Didn't even God rest after making the world?

"John, you are not to frolic with the Indians," Papa said at dinner that evening.

"But they're not doing any harm, Papa," John protested.

"Word has it the Pequot are trying to recruit the Narragansett for war against the English."

"Who says this is true?" I asked.

Papa sighed. There I went, questioning him again.

"A messenger came from Boston."

"How does Boston know what our Pequot are planning?" John said.

"They are not *our* Pequot," Papa corrected.

"That's true," I said. "They don't belong to us. They don't belong to anyone."

Papa rubbed his forehead. "Regardless, both of you will keep your distance."

"The English could learn from the Pequot," John said. "Like this game they play."

"Enough." Papa slapped the tabletop with his palm. "War is not a game, John. And while you are under my roof, you will be obedient."

John opened his mouth to speak but said nothing.

"His name is not John," I said. "His name is Running Wolf."

PATIENCE

A pall as heavy as an elk pelt fell over the village that December. We walked around each other without speaking, as if saying what we sensed was coming would bring on the calamity sooner.

I hadn't seen Minno in a week. Outside our stone wall women carried baskets laden with dried foods, skins and cooking pots as they readied for their march toward their winter camp by the Missituck River. I looked for Ayaks, but Minno had said he and the other men had gone ahead to hunt and make the longhouses ready for the cold months. His necklace was tucked under my shift, and my collar kept it hidden from Mother's vengeful eye.

After the Pequot broke camp and started east toward Missituck, I walked the meadow with Richard, checking the fences. Where a rail had come loose, we righted it. Where a stone had tumbled from a wall, we hefted it back into place.

"No walls will keep the Pequot off our property when they return in the spring," he said. "There's land aplenty in Connecticut—why do they have to trespass on ours?"

"They don't understand the word trespass, Richard," I said.

"They think just because they lived here before the Mayflower landed they're entitled to every square inch of wilderness. They have no understanding of civilization."

"Maybe not our civilization."

"They're wild, Sarah. They live like animals. How can you not see it?"

"You're right in that. Like the animals, they know how to survive. If you remember, half the Mayflower settlers died during the first winter and the others made it through because the Wampanoag natives kept them fed."

"The Pequot aren't like the Wampanoag. They're not to be trusted. Patience says they edge closer to Wethersfield every day." Over the last year, Richard had walked several times to Wethersfield to see Patience. A wedding in the near future would cheer us all up.

"I've told her to be careful around the savages," he said. "Reasoning with them is useless."

"Yes," I said. "Especially if you haven't tried."

When we returned to the house, Papa was waiting by the door. A frown darkened his face. Something was wrong.

"What has happened, Papa?" I asked.

"John Haynes has just arrived from Massachusetts."

"The Massachusetts Bay colony's new governor is in Hartford? Are the magistrates trying to work out a peaceful agreement with the natives?"

"I don't think agreement is what they have in mind." Papa pulled at his collar. His eyelids drooped. He looked weary.

"Sarah, go help your mother in the kitchen," he said.

I went as he bid but stayed close enough to overhear.

"Sit down, son," Papa said.

I peeked at them as I shelled beans. Papa examined his thumbnail and then locked his hands behind him and paced back and forth before the hearth.

Richard sat in front of the fireplace and braced himself on the bench, preparing for whatever Papa had to say. Wind whistled through the rafters. Outside snow began to fall.

"You know," Papa began, "some cattle and hogs have been killed with Indian arrows, and their dogs have maimed other livestock. The Pequot deny any guilt, of course. They blame wolves or strangers coming through town."

It would not have surprised me if Englishmen had shot the arrows to blame the natives. The Pequot braves were well out of our territory and in Missituck by now. Missituck must have been a distance of more than seventy kilometers traveling south toward the coast. It would take days to travel so far, and hogs would be a burden on such a trip.

"Those savages aren't above taking cows from our pastures," Richard said.

"Cows are the least of our worries." Papa pulled a chair forward and sat opposite Richard. He brought his fist to his mouth and studied the floor. After a moment he spoke.

"Two young women were taken from Wethersfield."

Richard turned to stone. "Taken? Taken where?"

"They were last seen in a pasture." Papa's voice broke and I thought he might weep. "Their bodies were found by the river."

"Bodies? You mean they drowned?"

"No," Papa said. "Stabbed. They were murdered."

Papa couldn't keep this outrage from me. I came from the kitchen.

"Who were the women?" I demanded.

Papa sighed. "One was a girl just arrived with her family." His shoulders slumped as if they were heavy as iron.

"The other?" Richard asked.

Papa rested his elbows on his knees and knitted his fingers together.

"Who was the other girl?" Richard's voice was insistent, angry. Still Papa stared at his hands. He worked his mouth but said nothing.

"It was Patience, wasn't it?" I said.

Papa gave a faint nod of his head.

"You are mistaken," Richard said. "I saw Patience just last week."

Papa looked at him. "There is no mistake, my son. I am sorry."

A giant boulder was rolling downhill and there was no way to halt it, no way to get out of its path. A boulder of retribution. A boulder of war.

"No!" Richard sobbed. Then he exploded. "Damn the Pequot!"

"You don't know it was Pequot," I said as calmly as I could. I couldn't imagine his grief.

"Who else would do such a thing?" he said.

I wished I had an answer. There were bad Englishmen, bad Dutchmen, bad Irish. There were bad Puritans, too. Grace did not extend to all men.

Richard pounded a fist into his palm. "The savages will pay for this."

"There are thousands of Pequot," Papa said. "We don't have enough men in Connecticut to deal with them. Governor Haynes is trying to work out an alliance with the Massachusetts Bay Colony."

"For fighting?" I said.

"It's the only way to keep our townships safe," Papa said. "The Pequot have killed John Oldham, too."

"Oldham, the English trapper?" Richard was on his feet.

"Everyone knows John Oldham was a drunkard and a cheat," I said. We had heard the rumors that Oldham got the natives drunk on strong spirits and then swindled them out of land and furs. They might have murdered him out of anger.

"No matter," Richard said. "He was a white man. He was one of us."

"Maybe he's the one who murdered—" I dared not say Patience's name for fear of upsetting Richard even more.

"What reason would Oldham have to do violence to women of his own race?" Papa asked.

"Maybe he meant to trade them for something," I said.

Richard looked at me, his face distorted with grief and anger. "Why would Oldham sell English women to the natives?"

"They have lost women to the pox," I said. "If Patience and the other girl had fought him—"

Some men—even Englishmen—considered women as objects to be traded or sold. But the Pequot kept no English women that I had seen.

"It had to be the Pequot," Richard said. "The governor is right—this calls for war."

"The Mohegan and Narraganset have no love for the Pequot," Papa said. "They will fight with us."

"Us?" I said.

Papa blotted his forehead with a handkerchief. "Captain Mason is looking for a hundred men."

"What sort of men?" said Richard.

"Good shots."

"Not you, Papa," I said. He was as spindly as a long-legged bird. He kept his thin hair cropped so that it sprung up like white feathers about his head. Coming to America had been his great hope, but it was the dream itself that was wasting him away.

Richard squared his shoulders. "I'll volunteer."

Papa nodded. "I'm a man of God, not a man of war. But if you feel moved to join, then you must go. I fear battle is the only way to peace."

"Peace through fighting? That defies reason," I said. "Find the guilty man and bring him to justice. Teach each side the ways of the other—there has to be a way besides war."

"There is no other way." Richard's jaw was clenched. "As God is my witness, war makes perfect sense."

———————

Most nights I went to bed believing everything to be fine. Then some mornings I awoke paralyzed with worry and the sense of a dreadful, indefinite future where nothing is certain. If I let myself, I might have gotten used to the unknown and not being able to control whatever was to unfold. But I didn't want to get used to it. I had to do something.

THE RECRUIT

On Sunday Reverend Hooker read from the first chapter of Genesis. "Be fruitful and multiply, and fill the earth, and subdue it, and have dominion over the fish of the sea and over the fowl of the air, and over every living thing that moveth upon the earth." Then he said that the Indians run across the grass like the foxes and other wild beasts and therefore they should be subject to English law. But it seemed to me that the natives didn't know the words "dominion over." I prayed that they would not suffer on account of English ignorance.

The war had already started in our house.

"You're not going to fight the Pequot, are you, Richard?" I was winding yarn from a spool.

"I can barely wait to load my musket," he said through gritted teeth.

John shook his finger at Richard. "A dog bites when it feels cornered. Be careful about cornering the Pequot." He broke a stick of kindling and poked it into the fire.

"When we first came to America, John, all you thought about was killing the Indians," Richard said.

"Did I?"

"As I remember, yes."

John stabbed at the embers with the poker. On the *Lyon* voyage he had talked of battles—thrilling, gory conflicts. But he wasn't a boy anymore. Those conflicts were text on the pages of history, harmless imaginings spurred by reading about the Greeks. Even if John had wanted to go to war, Papa would never have permitted it—he was too young, and we needed him to take care of farm chores while Richard was gone.

John leaned the poker against the hearth. "I was stupid," he said. "I know better now."

"Don't kill them, Richard," I said.

"I will do as I am commanded."

"Command or not, be true to yourself."

Richard hesitated. "I will be true—but I won't disobey orders."

"Will you make a pledge?" John said.

"I make no pledges except for Patience's sake."

I put aside the ball of yarn and heaved a sigh. "I have no doubt that whatever you do for whatever reason will follow you for the rest of your life."

Goodwives baked hardtack biscuits from bushels of corn supplied by the settlers—corn purchased from the very natives their men were going to fight. Soldiers packed their rucksacks with suet, salt, beans, rice, and cheeses, fueling themselves for the long march to Missituck.

Mother kneaded bread. She scoured the kettle. She washed bedclothes. And she performed all these chores as if time were running out. I was agitated. How should I have known what war meant? I understood the hunt, shooting an animal whose only defenses were tooth and claw. My own sling had taken down creatures to feed our stomachs. The natives had arrows and tomahawks against gunpowder and lead — where was the balance in that?

I found it hard to concentrate on my lessons or even on Chaucer's tales. If anyone should be going to war, it should be I — to stop it.

"How long do you think the war will last?" John asked. He had grown in the last months and we stood eye to eye.

"Help me fold this sheet." I handed him the end I had unpinned from the clothesline before the evening dew settled. I didn't want to talk about war.

"I wouldn't shoot an Indian even if Papa gave his blessing," John said.

"I'm glad to hear it," I said. "But Papa would never let either of us go anyway."

"You? A soldier? Ha!"

"What's funny about that? I marched with Ben and Christian when we came to Hartford. I can do anything Richard can do."

"Why would you want to fight the Pequot?" He dropped a corner of the sheet to tug at his britches.

"You're right — I wouldn't. Mind the sheet!" I lifted my end to keep the edge out of the dirt. "Looks like we're going to have to let out the seam in those knickers again."

"There's not much seam left. I guess they're ready for the rag bag."

"A shame." Then I had an idea. If Papa had a son a few years older than John, he wouldn't object to that son joining the other soldiers. I couldn't sit home and do nothing.

"Don't you have an old waistcoat you've outgrown?

"Mother set the buttons over and now she's going to sew a panel down the back." He puffed up his chest and tugged at his vest. "This one was Richard's. Waste not, want not."

I patted the sheet into the laundry basket. I could make good use of John's old waistcoat and as for his britches, there was sure to be some life left in them yet.

For a week I purloined biscuits from meals. The first ones were hard now and would have to be gnawed slowly or dunked in tea to soften them enough to chew. I tied them into a cloth with a few onions and some berries I dried under a glass. If I were a squirrel, I'd scavenge for food in the forest. If I were a bird, I'd carry only a worm or a bee to sustain me and watch the war from a safe distance.

But safety didn't concern me. The captains had convinced the Narragansett and Mohegan to be our allies. The two tribes were no more fond of the Pequot than were the English. If I could alert the Pequot about the rifles marching toward their longhouses, if I could hold back the English, Narraganset, and Mohegan soldiers, if I could save bloodshed on both sides, I intended to do it.

SPRING WIND

One night I dreamed of a rabbit, white as milk. She was caught in a snare. The more she struggled, the tighter the line became. The rope chafed her leg until it bled, scarlet staining her white coat. I watched her writhe, an unbearable sadness in her eyes. Try as I might, I could not ease her suffering. I awoke in a panic, my nightgown damp with sweat. If the dream carried a message, I shuddered to think what it might be.

"I'm leaving," Richard said.

Mother did not turn from the stove. I knew she was not in favor of Richard going to Missituck, but she dared not speak against Papa's wishes, even if it meant her son taking an arrow in the heart. She had washed and darned Richard's stockings and now folded them neatly into his rucksack along with a small jug of wild raspberry jam. As he walked up the road, Mother's eyes were like tender hands upon his back.

It was on my tongue to call Richard back, to ask him to think again about what he and the others were about to do. But that would be wasted effort. My brother's rage was aimed at the Pequot camp and nothing short of an almighty miracle would stop him. And yet, maybe something else could turn him around — something named Sarah Lyman.

Mother was at the town marketplace and John was out feeding the chickens. In his chest I found a wool shirt he hadn't worn in weeks. I slipped into it. The material was thick and loose enough so that my breasts wouldn't be noticed. I had barely noticed them myself until the last months. There was not yet much to hide, but John teased me so that I drew a curtain when I bathed. The shirt would serve me well.

John must have donned the new knickers Mother had sewn for him because his outgrown ones were slumped in a corner. I wiggled into them and tied a belt around the waist. John had grown indeed. One of his waistcoats hid my precious necklace, which would be safer around my neck than at home where Mother might find it. My field boots would have to do, and I thrust my feet into them and laced them up. Richard had left one of his hunting knives, and I took it and tied its leather sheath to my belt next to the sling. Lizzy's book of pilgrimage tales I pushed under my mattress. Most of it I knew by heart anyway.

When I pulled back my hair, it fell to my waist. As a girl I let my hair fly loose around my shoulders, but once I turned twelve, it was considered vain to wear it down in the village. When I went out, I twirled the tresses into a bun or braided and curled it around my head with a cap covering it. My hair was thick and as ashy colored as seasoned wood. Every two weeks I washed it in the scrubbing tub. I missed the evenings when I sat at my sister's knee and Phillis combed out the tangles. Drying my wet locks by the fire gave them a smoky scent that stayed in my pillow for days.

When I let my hair down now, I thought of Ayaks and his silky mane. What was the oil he used to give it such a beguiling aroma? If I cut my hair, would he take me for a fellow the next time he saw me? But there was a possibility that I would never see Ayaks again. I refused to think of it. Of course I would see him. And when I did, would he care about the length of my locks?

I took Mother's sewing scissors, cut off half a meter, and tied it back. My queue was now the length of Richard's. John's flatcap hung on a peg by the front door. I knitted it for him the year before, but he preferred an old beaver cap Richard had handed down to him. He wouldn't miss the flatcap. It was big enough to pull over my ears and if I kept my head down, the narrow brim would hide my face. I tied a kerchief around my neck and regarded myself in the looking glass. I did resemble a boy. The ruse might just work—it had to.

I wrote a note saying I was going to Wethersfield to give my condolences to Patience's family. I wasn't lying, really—I had every intention of doing just that—once I returned from Missituck. I left the note and slipped out the door without being seen.

It would take days for an army to hike the distance to Missituk, and the troops had several hours start on me. My legs were strong from farm work and without a long skirt to catch on brush, I could cut through the woods to save time.

Richard had joined the regiment in Hartford, and I watched as the group of men marched south along the river. Missituck was to the east and south, so the regiment's leader must have known a good place to cross.

It was late afternoon when I caught sight of the soldiers. I looked for Richard, but I recognized Christian first, Benjamin next to him. He stood a head taller than Benjamin and looked like a lanky scarecrow. Richard tramped behind them and I followed at the end of the company. I may have been foolish, but my determination prevented me from turning back.

A man rode up next to me and slowed his horse to a walk.

"What's your name, boy?" he said.

I bit my cheek. Name—I'd forgotten to give myself a name. August was my favorite month and brown was the hue of the earth.

"August, sir," I said. "August Browne."

"How old are you, August Browne?"

"I'm seventeen, sir." At least that was no lie.

"My name is Captain Mason, in charge of this company. Do you have a gun, soldier?"

"No, sir."

He pulled a musket from a saddlebag. "Know how to use this?"

"Yes, sir, I do." I tried to make my voice low and rough.

He handed the musket to me.

"Keep it clean. And be sure you don't fall behind." He saluted and rode down the line of marching men.

"Yes, sir, Captain Mason," I yelled after him. I perched the barrel over my shoulder and shuffled to keep up with the others.

At dusk we set up camp. Still we had not crossed the water. I wondered what Captain Mason had in mind. Men gathered firewood to make campfires and heat food for their suppers. I could have bagged a squirrel with my sling, but I dared not get close enough to a cook fire and raise questions. Night's chill set my teeth to rattling, and I huddled in my one scratchy blanket. I was a distance from Richard and his friends but close enough to hear them talking.

"At last," Christian said, "a chance to shoot at something besides raccoons."

"This time the prey will be shooting back," Benjamin said, "if not taking your scalp."

Christian tugged at a yellow cloth around his arm. "We have English trappers to thank for teaching the Indians about scalping. They traded Indian scalps to their enemies for food and wampum before the natives thought of it."

I didn't like talk of scalping. If I could help it, my brother and his friends would neither scalp nor be scalped.

"Why the armband?" Richard poked Christian's arm.

"In case of emergency — tourniquet, compress...."

"Flag of surrender?" Benjamin added.

"No," said Christian, "never that."

"You've brought a saber." Richard pointed to a sheath at Christian's side.

"An Indian can shoot five or six arrows in the time it takes to reload a rifle," he said. "We're better off in a hand duel."

"I'm hoping not to get that close," Benjamin said.

"Not going to run, are you?" said Christian.

Richard puffed out his chest. "We're here to fight, right Benjamin?"

Benjamin gave a quick nod. Running was an option he may have considered.

"Any idea what it feels like to be shot?" he asked.

I suddenly thought of my brother pinned to a tree by a razor-tipped arrow. Until now, our only foes were rocks in the path of the plow, weeds among the buckwheat, a stubborn knot that kept a log from splitting. I still didn't know why the governor wanted war. The Pequot were families just as we were — living in a different way maybe, but with the same spirit. For all that was holy, I couldn't see why the English didn't understand that.

AIM TRUE

At daybreak Captain Mason roused us from our bedrolls and ordered us to sprint back and forth across a meadow. The running warmed my feet and legs in this May morning chill. Even carrying the heavy musket, I could outrun half my company.

Afterward, we marched endlessly down forest paths, the river still to my left. In another day we'd be at the bay — and then what? The mouth of the river would be too wide to wade across, and I was not keen on swimming. Some of the boys were no older than I was. None of us knew how to be soldiers, but we followed the drills the best we could. I gnawed on a stale biscuit while I walked and wished Minno were here to show me where to find cress or mushrooms in the woods. But Minno was the enemy. With each step closer to Missituck, I marveled at how absurd that idea was. If I could have crossed the river, I might be able to reach the Pequot village ahead of the soldiers and warn her. But how?

On the second night, men set up tarpaulins for shelter, chopped firewood and toasted biscuits over campfires that sprang up like orange blossoms among the troops. Again I kept to myself and unfurled my bedroll a distance from the others. Most of the soldiers fell exhausted into their makeshift beds, but one man began singing "Over the Hills and Far Away." Another joined in on the lines

Courage, boys, 'tis one to ten,

But we return all gentlemen

All gentlemen as well as they,

Over the hills and far away.

When the singing faded, I heard Christian ask, "Do you think your father regrets sending you on this mission?"

"My father didn't send me." Richard's voice. "I came to punish the murderers for their savagery."

"Strong words, my friend," Christian said. "I'd be content to drive them out of Connecticut for good."

Benjamin broke in. "As much as I've grumbled about milking and fieldwork, I'd trade these marches for one more day on the farm." His voice trembled. None of us had any idea of what lay ahead.

"Ben, you'll be a hero when we're finished with these brutes," Christian told him.

Benjamin spoke to his boots. "If I live through it."

"Right," Christian said. "With luck we'll end this tussle without any one of us having a scratch."

I had no desire to be a hero. No matter what lay in front of us, I would hate to see anyone hurt. In fact, I intended to save as many native souls as I could. Weren't we all brothers and sisters under God — the Great White Rabbit? *Fortune is changeable,* Chaucer had written. Fortune had better cast its gaze in favor of us all.

The last words I remember hearing were, "We'd best catch some winks now."

Lying on the lumpy ground, I listened to the sounds of the wilderness—fires crackling, bullfrogs croaking, something skittering nearby. Each time I willed myself asleep, I awoke worried. In another day and a half we would reach Missituck. I needed a plan.

It was still dark when I heard voices—Captain Mason and a native. Narragansett, from the sound of him. He had returned from scouting ahead and reported seeing a gathering of Pequot braves farther down the river. They were in war paint.

In the dim light of early dawn, birds trilled through the fog as if they had no inkling of the peril ahead. I sat up and pulled on my flatcap.

"Be vigilant now, men," Captain Mason called.

Richard rolled Benjamin over. "Up now, lad," he said.

"Is there breakfast?" Benjamin knuckled an eye socket.

"Ha," Richard laughed. "Not unless you scoop an acorn along the warpath."

"Pack up," Christian said, tugging at his armband. "Captain says we're in for our first battle."

Still groggy, I rolled onto my feet and fell into a slow trot behind the others. The musket bounced on my shoulder and limbs caught my cap and tilted it on my head. Captain Mason cautioned us to look out for caves in the rock walls and eyes peering from heavy brush. All my senses were on alert.

Spring wildflowers had broken through the damp ground. Violets, trillium, trout lily. The delicate flowers quivered as we trudged past. Benjamin lost his balance and stepped on a trillium blossom, crushing it. How little it took to destroy innocence.

The captain ordered us to halt at the edge of a grove. We were to make no sound. The silence was eerie, and I thought of Minno sneaking up on the mink to kill the animal for its pelt. I found some smooth rocks, reached down and dropped three into my pocket. Then I knelt and checked my musket. It was loaded, though I would refuse to fire it. I lay on my stomach a short distance from Benjamin and rested the barrel on a rock, sighting into the haze. Every muscle was coiled tight. More waiting. Time stretched out like long shadows, and soft snowflakes floated lazily down and melted.

At last, from down the line came the command, "Steady, steady." Still I heard nothing, not even the pathetic chirp of an insect. Even the birds were still. At least the onions I'd eaten the night before kept the bugs away.

Through the fog I heard a wild "Ayeeee!"

Suddenly, Pequot warriors swarmed like angry hornets, their stingers poised to fly from their bows. Their faces, arms, chests were painted yellow, orange, red.

"Fire!" Captain Mason called.

"The game is afoot," Benjamin murmured, screwing up his nerve.

Guns went off around me and the acrid smell of burnt powder singed my nostrils. Arrows zipped about like a hail of thorns. Smoke rocketed from Benjamin's rifle and a brave fell back. Benjamin lifted himself to one knee for reloading.

"Ben!" I hollered. "Get down!"

It was too late. He grunted as a shaft pierced his shoulder. I crawled to him and saw the arrow had gone clean through. He rolled in pain, but I grabbed his boots to steady him. Ben was hefty but somehow I found the strength to drag him behind a ledge and cradled his head in my arms to keep his weight off the shoulder.

Richard crawled to us and looked at me as if he'd seen a ghost.

"Lord in Heaven," he said. "How did you get here?"

"The same way you did," I said.

"Go home, Sarah. Go home now." His voice had venom and I was afraid he would strike me.

I shook my head. Dressed as an English boy, I'd be an easy target and Richard knew it.

"All right, but you stay with Ben." This was one time I listened to my brother. He bit off the cap of his powder pouch and poured a healthy dose into the musket, then jammed in the steel rod to tamp it down. The barrel steamed from its last firing.

Benjamin groaned and slapped at the arrow as if it were a scorpion.

"This is the crack of doom," he grunted through a jaw clenched in pain. Shakespeare himself could not have been more poetic at such a time.

"Be still," I said and squeezed his good hand. He bit his lips between his teeth.

I peered over the mossy ledge. The English were swinging rifle butts, slashing with sabers, ducking tomahawks. It looked as if wild men were fighting wild men, both sides howling in frenzy.

"You've got a single shot, Richard," Benjamin grunted. "Make your aim sure."

Richard wiped his eyes with his sleeve and rested the musket atop the ledge, sighting near a flashing sword. The swordsman's arm was girded with a yellow cloth. Christian was matching skills with a Pequot just as another approached him from behind, tomahawk raised.

I ripped the sling from my belt, reached into my pocket and settled a rock into the cup.

"Stay still, Ben," I said, and I propped him against a sapling. Kneeling behind my brother, I raised my arm, whirled the sling three times, and let the stone fly. Just as the missile hit the Indian's arm and knocked the tomahawk from his fist, Richard's musket fired. The native stayed on his feet and reached again for his tomahawk, but Christian was quick with his saber.

A life saved, a life taken. So this was what war was about.

Richard lowered his gun, thinking his was the shot that saved Christian.

"That's for Patience," he breathed.

As suddenly as the Pequot had appeared, they vanished into the thickets. On the battlefield, uniformed bodies lay next to half-naked ones like tired men resting, some red with paint and some with blood. In the silence, my ears rang from the explosion of gunfire.

THE RIVER

I broke off one end of the arrow, pulled it from Ben's shoulder, and hoped the natives had not dipped the tips in mulberry or another poison. Then I pressed the wound with my neckerchief to staunch the bleeding. Christian produced a pouch of liquid—spirits, I guessed—and poured some into the wound. Then he lifted the pouch to Ben's lips and Ben took several good swallows. Richard ripped a strip of bedroll to fashion a sling. We would have to leave Ben behind. He had lost too much blood to continue the march.

"You stay behind and tend to Ben," Richard said.

I protested. "We've got to get Ben to a physician." A doctor was at least a day's ride away, and there were other wounded men in the field.

Captain Mason rode toward us and halted his horse.

"The wounded will be sent back," he said. "You able men will march forward."

I helped Ben to his feet. He leaned on me as I walked him to a wagon already loading with bleeding men.

"You'll be all right," I said. "We'll see you back in Hartford."

Ben only nodded, too weak to speak.

Through the forest my feet fell into a rhythm: one-two-three-four. Five-six-seven-eight. When I reached twenty-four, I began again. How many steps had I taken over the last days? Twenty thousand? Twenty million? It seemed to me that we were still heading south, not in the direction of Missituck.

Captain Mason ordered the militia — ninety of us — to march in twos where the trail allowed and single file through the densest sections, always keeping sight of the soldier ahead. Christian walked in front of me and Richard behind, so close he stepped on my heels. His hovering annoyed me. I was tempted to break free from the ranks and from my brother's protection. I could have run ahead and marched with the Narragansett warriors. Several natives led the way and others crept through the woods near the trail. I was glad for their company, but I wasn't aware of what the Pequot had done to make them enemies — enemies they intended to overpower. And then what? Take them prisoner?

Tension hung in the air among the soldiers and braves, all of us alert and watchful for ambush. The Pequot must have known what the English had planned. I couldn't blame them for trying to protect themselves.

If Ayaks had been in the battle, I hadn't recognized him. Would he have found an excuse not to fight the British? Would he have thought of me? I wished him to be far away, with his father at the Dutch settlement, perhaps. And where was Minno? I had to push those thoughts from my head. I had to stay focused.

Toward dusk the ground became blessedly soft under my boots. Trees gave way to open sky, and tall grasses grew from marshy mud. I knew the scent of saltwater from so many months by Massachusetts Bay, but saltwater meant we should have been in Missituck by now, not beside our own Connecticut river. Maybe the skirmish with the natives had changed Captain Mason's mind. Maybe he would call off the attack. I held onto that thought with some relief. But the relief was short lived.

This place must have been where the river emptied out, freshwater meeting salty. What richness was here — long-legged birds standing up to their knees or soaring overhead, orange flowers among the reeds. And all sorts of bugs I swiped away with a free hand.

Beyond the marsh I caught sight of tall masts of English schooners afloat in deeper water, their sails lowered. Smaller rowing boats waited, watching for us.

"What is this?" I asked Richard. "Are we to board ships?"

It was Christian who answered.

"The Pequot think we've given up the fight," he said. "Captain Mason's plan is to sail east to Narragansett Bay and anchor there. Then we'll march west to the village." Christian puffed up his chest as if proud of the captain's ingenuity.

Richard added, "Captain Underhill's regiment will meet us in Rhode Island, raising our numbers to five hundred, counting English and native soldiers. The captain estimates a thousand savages among the Pequot but if we approach from the west, they won't be expecting an attack."

I wished no harm to the English, but at least the difference in number might give the Pequot a fair chance.

"Sarah," Richard said, "this is your last chance. I insist you give up this lunacy and go home."

"Lunacy is the right word for what the English are about to do." I tried to control my temper. Even though I didn't fancy boarding a ship that looked very much like our old vessel *Lyon*, I was not going to turn back, no matter what my brother said. "And Richard," I said, "my name is August—August Browne. Now let's get to the ship."

When the ship set sail, I fairly collapsed from exhaustion but I wouldn't let on to Richard and Christian. I would have marched the soles of my boots off if I'd had to. A night on the deck revived me, and when the ship dropped anchor in Narragansett Bay, I was ready.

That day we marched what must have been twenty kilometers through sandy terrain. We had to be close now to Missituck. Captain Mason stopped the regiment by a brook and ordered us to stay low and keep mute. We were not to light campfires in case the natives should see the flames and smell the smoke, and we were not to unfurl our bedrolls. I couldn't have slept anyway.

The order to move forward was just hours away. I settled down near Richard and Christian. A blue mist hovered low above the fields, and the trees cast long purple shadows under a bright crescent moon. The brook—a small river really—shimmered like a silver dragon. No doubt longhouses squatted in a clearing just across the water, wigwams scattered among them. A settlement of Pequot women, children, young braves, and elders asleep in their homes — Minno. Ayaks.

"Richard," I said, my voice low.

"What is it?"

"We can't attack. We can't—"

"I told you to go back to Hartford," he snarled. "You should have listened to me."

"I mean, there's no point. The Pequot have traveled far enough from Hartford. What threat are they to us here?"

Richard took a breath and blew it out. "Even if I tried, I could no more stop the attack than I could halt a herd of stampeding buffalo."

I could hear his teeth grinding together. He spat.

"But I don't want to stop it," he said. "If we are to survive in Connecticut, the Pequot have to be extinguished."

Had I heard Richard correctly? "Extinguished? You mean killed? What about the commandment — Thou shalt not—?"

"This is war," he hissed. His voice was edged with fury. "The Bible is filled with battles. The Israelites fought the Amalekites and the Midianites, and you said yourself that David slew Goliath."

"But invading at night while the natives are sleeping is not honorable or morally right, even in war."

"Most of the braves are scouting, looking for English soldiers. No one will be guarding the houses. This is our best chance."

I thought again of Minno. "There are children in those houses. Their mothers, too. The women and children have done us no harm."

"The Pequot leave destruction and terror in their wake. You have no idea how wicked these people are."

"Yes — people. People just like us."

"Not like us, no." He shook his head. "Read the Psalms. 'Let death steal over them for evil is in their dwelling place and in their heart.' There is nothing godly about them."

I tried to keep my voice down, but I couldn't let Richard win this argument.

"If you are so godly, you should read your Bible more closely, especially the book of Hebrews. 'The Lord will judge his people.' Who are you and the other soldiers to pass judgment over the Pequot?"

He planted his hands on my shoulders. "Listen to me now — when we get the command to march, I want you to stay right here. No matter what happens, don't go near the village. I'll come back for you later."

I didn't answer. How could I sit by and do nothing?

I had to think.

If I could sneak away, I could alert the elders. But would the elders welcome the message? To them, I would be the enemy, an English boy traveling with armed soldiers. A boy who was himself armed. No — I would carry only the sling. Minno would tell the natives that I was a friend. But the English would still attack. I couldn't possibly steal all their muskets and sabers. And there were the Mohegans fighting with the colonists. It was unavoidable — there was going to be death on both sides.

Richard was right — it would take an act of God to stop this war. And so I prayed to the Great White Rabbit and to the Puritan God. Surely one of them — or both together—could make the soldiers realize the wrong they were about to commit.

The brook's gurgling water was the only thing that calmed me. The men must have felt the pressure, too. They batted at mosquitoes. They checked their muskets and fidgeted.

It was near midnight when Captain Mason passed the word to gather ourselves. We were to take only our weapons and leave our gear at the camp. Dozens of men carried unlit torches with their guns.

Unlit? When would they light them? To see what?

"Stay still," Richard said. "And don't go near the river. I'll come for you after sunrise."

I blinked at him but didn't answer. My charge was to obey the orders of Captain Mason, not my brother.

Mohegan braves led the soldiers upstream. I put down my musket. It was a clumsy, useless thing, and I would not fire it against the Pequot. When the men were a good distance off, I followed.

Under moonlight a Mohegan crouched, motioning the militia into the river. There was a sandbar where the water was shallow enough so they could hold their muskets over their heads and wade in up to their waists.

I waited on the bank, listening to the noise of the river. The ripples seemed to speak to me in ancient languages. *Salām, wetaskiwin, śānti, sipala.* I had not heard the words before, but I knew what they meant. Peace, the river was singing. Peace, peace, peace. The sound was of a high-pitched rushing as water tumbled over itself. Under the surface, a low music of deeper water moving sluggishly over rocks. I swirled with the river, frustration and fear wrestling with desperation, hope, and a growing panic. I knew what was coming, but I could not abandon the Pequot.

Slowly I stepped into the water. Cold flooded my boots and shocked me alert. My feet went numb. This far south the water was salty, and I had trouble keeping my feet on the bottom. If I didn't pay attention, I would float downstream and out to sea, maybe all the way to Virginia. I was tempted to give in to the water's force, to let it take me away instead of pushing me toward what felt like doom.

DAMNATION

When I reached the village, men were scurrying, propping logs against the doors of the longhouses, piling twigs and branches against the walls. Captain Mason lit torches and passed the fire among the soldiers. Someone shoved a torch into my hands. This was good, I thought. I would be able to see the natives when we brought them out of their houses and maybe I would find Minno. If we were going to take the natives captive, at least she would see a friendly face.

A soldier soused the branches and twigs with lamp oil. Flammable oil. They were going to touch the torches to the branches. They were going to turn the longhouses into ovens. They were going to roast the Pequot alive.

Before we roasted a pig, we slit its throat. Before we fried a chicken, we wrung its neck. For the sake of compassion, the suffering of animals was kept to a minimum. But the soldiers intended to make the natives suffer unbearable torment.

I tore to the nearest longhouse, grabbed twigs and tossed them away. Someone gripped my arm and pulled me back. Two men held me as I kicked and writhed to get free. The captain waved his arm and torches set the sticks ablaze. Dry grass caught and crept around the buildings like bright snakes.

"No!" I cried out. And again, "No!"

Richard had burned wasp nests this way. But these were no wasps.

The fire crackled and sputtered. I willed it to go out. But the tinder ignited and swept the walls—an angry light, an evil light. Smoke escaped through chinks in the wood and flames leaped into the night, sending up red sparks like tiny planets flung into the darkness.

I heard bawling. Coughing. The thud of bodies hurling themselves against the doors. But logs wedged the doors closed. How could the wood catch so quickly? The heat of the fire mixed with the reek of meat—not pig, not calf nor venison, but the awful stench of burning human flesh. It must have been the same stench of witches burned alive at the stake. But the Pequot had committed no witchcraft.

The fire ate at the doors, devouring the wood until it was brittle enough to break through. Women burst into the night, some with their hair afire, running, stumbling. Some carried babies in their arms, shielding them from the fire with their own bodies. Could they all burn and still survive? Please, I prayed to whatever power ruled the heavens, please let them survive.

A girl broke free of the inferno, a girl with long braids. Around her neck, a knitted scarf, the ends alight, her bare back blistering with heat.

"Minno—Minno!" I wrestled free of the men and ran toward her but someone yanked me back. My cap went flying and I heard my shirt rip. Gunpowder burst from muskets. Swords flashed. In the chaos of yelling and moaning and musket fire, I saw bodies—hundreds of bodies—fall and lie still.

I stumbled away from the damnation, the stink of eternal hellfire, and found a sturdy tree. Leaning against the trunk, I rested my head on my knees and thought of the eagles I had seen soaring above the river in Hartford. Their eyes searched the water, looking down for fish they could clutch in their talons. They belonged in the air, not below the water's surface, but they would dive for their dinner and for a few brief seconds, the two worlds would connect. I had made a connection with the native world, but I didn't belong to it. Now I had been part of its destruction.

The necklace dangled between my thighs and I gripped it as if the shell and beads could stop this nightmare. When I looked at what was left of the village, embers glowed red and the ground gleamed like lava. A volcano eruption was an act of nature, but this was the carnage of men.

"Ayaks," I said aloud. "Wherever you are, be safe." And then somehow he was on his knees next to me, his face close to mine. I could smell his sun-drenched skin, the sweet oil in his hair. As he bent over me, strands fell forward and brushed my cheek. I tried to speak, to tell him to run for his life. But I couldn't make a sound. There was a roaring in my head. Or maybe it was the roaring of soldiers and the angry fire devouring its prey.

"I'm sorry, I'm sorry, I'm sorry," I sobbed.

His eyes glowed yellow. Wolf eyes. Fierce and wild. A wolf in a pit, caught, facing his destroyers.

"Go," I said. "Go. Now. Quickly."

When he put his palm on the necklace, the heat from his hand went through the shell and into my chest. A shot rang out. The musket ball hit the tree above his head and splintered the bark. I shoved him toward the forest.

"Ayaks, go!" I yelled. He took one last look at me and leaped into the night.

The thunder of firing and weeping went on as if in some insane festival. Smoke climbed like phantoms into a starry sky. Prayer was useless now. God had abandoned us — all of us. I willed the horror to end, but it would never be over — not that night, not for years, not for centuries.

I turned and pressed my shoulder against the tree as my stomach erupted. When my gut was empty, I sat on the ground, hot from the fires. Arms on my knees, head on my arms, I didn't look up again until Richard found me.

"It's over" was all he said.

Som tyme an end ether is of every dede, the Knight's Tale had said at the finish of Palamon's war. A time comes when end there is of every deed. The English had done their deed. The village was nothing but blackened and smoldering pieces of wood and charred bodies of the dead, victims of a cowardly massacre. Pequot children, young people and elders.

A few dozen Englishmen had tomahawk wounds, but I had no sympathy for them. The soldiers left standing gaped stupidly at the devastation of their work.

Richard wandered away. In that moment he was not my flesh and blood. He was a stranger and I wanted no part of him.

GHOSTS

My head throbbed. I looked around for a way to escape the madness of this night, but I had lost my sense of direction. Which way was the river?

Some wisdom told me stay where I was and wait for first light. I lost track of time until an orange blush broke through the trees. Then I rose to my feet and began walking with the light at my back.

When I came to a wide river, I trudged along the bank in the direction I believed was north. Eventually the river became a stream narrow enough to wade across. Hours later, daylight faded and I lumbered forward in the dark. When I stumbled, I slept where I fell. I had no fear of danger. What could happen that was worse than what I had witnessed?

Night became day and day night but by luck I found my way home — although home would never be a comfort for me again. When I saw Mother wringing her hands, I wondered who the strange woman was, her dark hair now streaked with silver, her mouth drawn into a thin line of worry.

"Sarah," she said. "Sarah, thank the Lord."

The Lord — a word that no longer had meaning.

"I'm tired," I said.

"What were you thinking? You're only a girl." Mother wrung her apron in her hands. "You had no business — "

"When I see a wrong," I interrupted, "I cannot sit by and do nothing."

"You could have been slain." She held her hand to her cheek.

"Yes, there was killing. Too much killing."

"It was war, Sarah."

I was hot, but Mother drew a shawl around my shoulders. Either I had grown taller or she had shrunk. She looked so frail.

"War is about equal opponents battling each other," I said, "not about sneaking in at night and committing murder."

Mother straightened and turned toward the kitchen. "In war someone wins and someone loses. The governor was not about to let us lose."

Us — the English, she meant. How could I ever again be one of "us"?

I followed her to the kitchen. I wouldn't back down where this argument was concerned.

"Hundreds lie dead because of who they are, hundreds who had not raised a hand against us." I slammed my knapsack down. "A whole village — burned. How can that be victory?"

"I'm sorry you saw that." How could Mother sound so composed? "I'll draw you a bath and make you something to eat. After you've rested, you'll feel better. In time you'll see there was no other choice."

"What we choose determines who we are. I am afraid, Mother, to see what we — what all of us — have become."

After I had bathed and eaten a little, Papa came in. He, too, seemed years older. Had I been gone so long? Where he stood, I saw he was leaning on a cane.

"What can I say to you, Sarah?"

"There is nothing you can say. But you can weep, Papa. You might weep."

"In honesty, I did not know it would be this way."

"You know how it went, then?" I said.

He nodded. "Even if I wept, no measure of sadness will cover this act. Even the cries of the Almighty would not change anything."

I fell into bed and was instantly asleep. But sleep gave me no respite. In nightmares wailing specters flew into me, through me, as if my own body were nothing but smoke. Sharp-tooth gargoyles, crouching wolves, scorching fire blistering my skin. Minno with flaming braids. And always just before I woke, the face of Ayaks.

In the days that followed, I walked about as if in a trance. Food had no flavor. Everything tasted of ashes. Richard returned, but how could I sit at table with him as if I had not witnessed the fires of hell? When Papa spoke to him, Richard acted as if he did not hear. The musket fire and cries of anguish had made him deaf.

I refused to go to Sunday meetings. No minister could explain to me how God could allow the butchery that took place at Missituk. God Himself was silent, and I believed that He, too, had retreated into the shadows of grief.

Papa spent more time in town. One evening when he returned he reported that in the final tally, six hundred Pequot had died. The natives who escaped were hunted down and handed to Narragansett and Mohegan tribes. They were not to use the name Pequot ever again, and they would become slaves to their captors. I knew that even if Minno had survived, for her slavery would be worse than death.

Governor Haynes declared the war at Missituck a success. All of Hartford rejoiced that the Pequot would not be returning to our borders. No, not all of Hartford. In the Lyman house there was no joy.

I wondered if Richard could look across the pastures as I did and see the golden ghosts weaving mats and fishing nets. The settlers tore down the wigwams, but the souls of the Pequot were there still. I heard them. I smelled their campfires burning. I watched the children dance.

REVENGE

It was mid-June and the gardens wanted planting. The seeds would barely have time to sprout and yield their bounty before first frost. I had given up John's knickers and put on a skirt and apron again. Combing my fingers through the seeds in my apron pocket, I thought how each was a tiny world waiting to come to life, to give its offering and then wither and die. Life for the seeds was a slow and peaceful process. It should have been so with humans. Minno had offered me her friendship, and what did I give to her? A fiery death. She had no chance to grow old.

While I whacked the hoe at a clump of dirt, John darted recklessly over the meadow. Sometimes he seemed a young man and at other times he was still a child. I had forgotten what it was like to feel so carefree.

Suddenly he stopped.

I followed his gaze to the field's edge where a brave stood as if sculpted from stone. Orange war paint streaked his forehead, his cheeks and the ridge of his nose. Yellow smeared across his chest and down his arms. But his shining hair was loose. The wind lifted it like falcons shaking their wings. In one motion he scooped

John up as if he were not more than a bag of grain. In a flash the native's tomahawk was out of his breeches and raised above his head, aimed straight for the neck of my younger brother.

I thought maybe I was dreaming. The sky held no cloud to filter the sun, and the brightness nearly blinded me. My lips tasted of salt. My arms were damp with sweat. No, I couldn't be dreaming.

Somehow I flew across the field and yanked my brother from the native's grip.

"Go to the house, John." I shoved him behind me and looked up into a face of anguish, the face of Ayaks. A wild odor came from him, as if a bear had run across a continent, as if all fish had jumped from the sea in one leap, as if he had dug a tunnel to the center of the earth. It was the awful scent of hatred. It was the smell of death.

His tomahawk hung in the air, the sky blue around it, blue holding the weapon aloft, only blue keeping the glinting blade from cleaving my flesh.

"Revenge won't bring them back, Ayaks," I said. "Don't be like the English."

Moments passed, or centuries—I could not tell which. Tides rose and fell, the moon waned and waxed, night fell and dawn silvered the sky once again, and still the tomahawk poised high in his grip.

I refused to flinch. Slowly I reached my fingers to the hooks of my bodice and opened it, exposing my chemise. With both hands I yanked the cotton until the cloth tore so that my breasts were bare, the necklace's abalone shell glistening purple against my pale skin.

"If my death gives recompense for the evil wrought upon your people," I said, "then bury your hatchet in my heart."

If Ayaks didn't understand what I had said, I'm sure he knew my meaning. The tomahawk quivered above his sinewy arm. Then his grip loosened, and his arm fell to his side. With his other hand, he touched my neck, and I lifted my chin toward him. His warm hand slid down to my breast. In his deep brown eyes, I understood his agony.

"Come," he said and tossed his head toward the forest. "Come away with me."

I shook my head slowly. "My father is old. My place is — here." A sob rose in my throat. I couldn't leave. Ayaks couldn't stay. I had never felt so torn.

I lifted the necklace. I had grown so used to the weight of its beads that when I no longer had it around my neck, I felt as if I would float upward and disappear into the clouds.

When I held the necklace out to Ayaks, he made no gesture to accept it, but he did not recoil when I looped it over his head and centered the abalone shell at his chest.

We stood together, my pale face close to his painted one. My arms ached to be around his neck.

Suddenly behind me I heard Richard yell, "Get away from her!"

Ayaks looked up and I dared to turn my head. Richard was standing in front of the house, musket in his hand. As he raised the gun, Papa came out and halted behind him.

"Put the gun down," Papa said, his voice even and stern.

Richard sighted down the musket barrel aimed straight at Ayaks.

"Put it down, son." Papa's voice was tender now. "There has been too much killing."

I saw the musket tremble and then like a retreating rattlesnake, it lowered its venom toward the ground. When I tore my eyes back to Ayaks, my vision blurred as I watched him vanish across the meadow like a wisp of vapor.

Mother came out with a shawl and wrapped it around my body. As I walked past Richard and Papa, I felt as if I had lost everything. Nothing mattered to me—not my family, not the lovely new Lyman house, not even Connecticut. When Ayaks left, he took my spirit.

I went upstairs to my room and threw myself onto my bed. Not until then did I let go of my pride and allowed the tears to overtake me.

THE DECLINE

Mother and I planted flower seeds and nurtured the sprouts with compost. What a miracle that in a single season nature could turn rotting vegetation into fragrant beauty. The Hartford gardens had not the splendor of the English countryside, but the flowers gave our house a touch of beauty.

I needed beauty. There had been so much horror. Except for a few Narragansett allowed by the town council, no natives came near our settlement after the war, as they called it. The death of Patience and her friend was filed away as a barbarian act of savages. The English soldiers were lauded as heroes.

Richard walked the pastures, dragging his hand along the fence, craning his neck to watch the sky. He finished his chores alone, never asking for help. When I offered to do the milking, he turned and went out to the barn without a word. He left the slaughter of the chickens to John and never hunted again. When Papa asked, Richard told him he had lost his musket. Papa offered him another, but he said he didn't need a gun.

One afternoon I found him at the stone wall, staring into the forest. When I came to him, he didn't speak. I searched for something to talk about that would interest him.

"It's September already and harvest is nearly done," I said. He didn't answer, so I tried again. "Ruby still pulls hard at the plow for such an old ox." I thought he might have given the slightest nod of his head.

"And did you notice how straight the rows are?" I said. "No curlicues."

A nod for certain this time.

I didn't blame Richard. I might have told him I understood his misery, but the words had too heavy a weight and I couldn't find the strength to utter them.

We stood together a few moments in the morning quiet.

Finally, he spoke. "I don't feel hatred toward the Pequot."

"I'm glad of that, Richard."

"Captain Mason said the hand of God guided our victory that night." He leaned on the fence and looked at the ground. "More like the hand of Satan. Don't you think so, Sarah?"

"I don't know."

He fell silent again.

I pressed my hand to his back. "Don't blame yourself, Richard."

He shuddered. His torment must have pressed on him like an anvil.

Leaves were turning red and gold on the maples and birches, honoring the change of seasons as if disaster had not occurred. Maybe my brother would come back to life, too.

For months Papa sat vigil by a window, looking over the fields. I brought his meals to him there, what little he would eat. Before the sun had set, he was already abed. I knew he was dying.

Mother called a doctor to tend to him—although doctor wasn't the proper word. Any man with money could claim a medical license. Bleeding him and applying compresses of herbs did no good. The doctor could not heal old age. Papa was nearly sixty.

When the doctor left, either John or I sat at Papa's bedside and read aloud to him from the Good Book. Other times we talked of summer's harvest or next spring's planting. We never spoke of the Pequot. When he had the energy, Papa told the story of how he met Mother, and each time was as if he were telling it anew.

"She had a small stand at the market next to her father's pumpkins and carrots." A smile lighted his gray face. "Oh, she was pretty, her lips as rosy as her cheeks, and her hair done up in a dark braid hanging over one shoulder. The aroma of her mince and squash pies made my mouth water."

He moistened his lips with his tongue as if tasting the pies so many decades later.

"Every Saturday for a month, I bought a mince pie just to visit with her. I always gave the pie away. The very sight of her made me too full to eat."

Papa's speech was halting. He stopped to take a few labored breaths and then he started again, telling how her father told him that he might as well come around to the house instead of taking up patron space in the marketplace. The talks became courting and before he knew it, Papa was eating her mince pies regularly. She still made the best mince pies he'd ever tasted, he said. I agreed.

I listened but never mentioned my greatest worry — life without Papa. We had always looked to him to make decisions. His was the voice of authority. Who would fill his shoes when he was gone? Richard was Papa's favorite among his children. But Richard was in no frame of mind to lead a family.

A rattle came from Papa's chest. I wiped saliva from the corners of his mouth with a handkerchief.

"I have no fear of death," he said.

"Hush, Papa. Please don't talk of dying."

"Death is even now at the foot of my bed, beckoning me like a welcoming host."

I leaned toward him. How could I explain away my willfulness, and how could he understand that I was who I was, not who he wanted me to be — meek and docile? If he only knew that despite my obstinacy, I loved him. We had spoken of seasons and of crops, but we had never mentioned love.

"Tell me what I can do for you, Papa," I said.

He smiled faintly and said, "Send me Richard."

THE WILL

I found Richard still in bed, even though daylight filtered through the window shutters. For a moment I thought he had plunged himself into purgatory. How long would he have to live the lie about what happened at Missituck?

"Papa is asking for you," I said.

He had avoided our father. Papa had wanted him to go to war, even approved the fighting. My father was a good citizen and supported the governor's decrees, but the massacre of the Pequot was not Papa's fault. Richard should not place blame on him.

When I opened the shutters, he shielded his eyes with an arm.

"You'd best come now," I said. "There's not much time."

He sat up and tossed his legs over the side of the bed, but he didn't rise.

"If it will help," I said, "I'll go with you."

Papa's body made barely a ripple under the coverlet. He smelled of decay, of something finding its way back to the earth.

"Get the quill," Papa said.

Richard shuffled through the desk and found ink and paper. When he was ready, he told Papa to begin.

Papa licked his lips. "Richard Lyman, Senior. Last Will and Testament."

Richard showed no emotion and scribed the words as if someone else were writing them.

"To my wife, I leave the house, the household items, a third of the land, and the cattle." Papa stopped and closed his eyes. It seemed to pain him to speak, but shortly he began again.

"My eldest son Richard shall receive the remaining two-thirds of the land."

"Thank you, my lord." Richard's voice was barely above a whisper.

Because Phillis had William to take care of her, Papa left her just ten shillings.

"Sarah is to receive forty pounds to sustain her until she marries."

"Which I expect is a goodly way off," Richard added with an attempt at humor. Papa struggled a pitiful grin.

Marriage? No. I would live frugally and find a way to earn my own living. I would not pledge my life to any man. Any man except Ayaks. Where was he? How was he faring without his people? Did he hate me? I could not have borne his hatred.

I thought Papa had drifted to sleep, but in a few moments he spoke again.

"To my youngest son John I leave thirty pounds to be paid at twenty-two years of age unless —" He coughed and brought a handkerchief to his lips. "Unless he causes trouble for his mother, at which time she should keep the money."

"Fair enough," Richard said.

Papa may have been approaching the gates of heaven, but he was still in charge.

THE RESOLUTION

Puritans did not observe religious services at funerals. Prayer, we believed, should not be used for those already deceased. And so no words, neither of sorrow nor of faith, were spoken over Papa's body. Instead, our family and neighbors followed the coffin to the gravesite in silence. The only sound that spring day was the tolling of the church bell. Papa would have approved of that simple dignity.

At home Mother covered the looking glass and paintings with cloths and closed the window shutters. She would not mourn her beloved in any other way. Papa at last had found the comfort of which he had so long dreamed.

After we had laid him to rest, Papa's name was carved on a stone column in the Centre Church of Hartford with others as founders of the Connecticut Colony. Hundreds of years hence, visitors would find my father's name there. But there were no names of Pequot natives inscribed on the column. It was as if the attack at Missituck had erased them from the earth.

Within the following year, Mother took ill and wasted no time in joining Papa in heaven. She seemed happy to go.

As Chaucer said in the Knight's tale, *By processe and by lengthe of certeyn yeres Al stinted is the moorninge and the teres.* For the Lyman children, too, time had dried our tears and healed our mourning. We needed to face whatever came next.

John said he'd had enough of Connecticut. I suspected the Pequot spirits haunted my younger brother as they did me. I yearned to see my sister and her family. And perhaps my old friend Lizzy would have arrived from England and was waiting for me.

John and I packed our belongings and got ready to begin the long trek back to Boston.

"Come with us, Richard," I said.

"This is Father's and Mother's resting place" he said. "I belong here."

I hugged him for a long time.

He pulled away and gave a faint smile. "Remember the narrow path we took through the forest?"

"I do," I said.

"Now that path is wide enough for a carriage."

It would be an easier journey this time. Richard had bought a horse for us and harnessed it to a wagon.

"We'll look for you to come to Boston," John said. But I knew Richard would stay in Hartford. It was what Papa would have wanted.

We left the livestock with Richard—a cow and calf, a heifer and a bull, a goat and two kids, eight hogs and a sow. I took a chest, a kettle, a skillet and an iron pot. We had four Lyman platters, and Richard wrapped two, one to give to Phillis and the other for me, along with two tablecloths and some linen napkins. He kept the fireplace tools, a sword and belt, and two firelock pieces. I had no need of the tools—two scythes, two ladders, a churn, two wedges, two saws and some chisels. Richard gave one of the two axes to John.

I told my brothers that I needed some time alone and went to the meadow. Perched on a boulder by the woods, I thought how Papa had planted our family seeds in American soil, seeds already sprouting into a lineage that would prosper in the New World. Richard would find another love and raise a family to carry on the Lyman name. John would grow up and sire children, too. They would be strong and healthy and, knowing John, they would be peaceful men and women who respected the living spirit in all things.

Minno had told me that the natives call the spirit manitou. Manitou is in the trees and the rivers, in the animals of the forest and in the hearts of the people who inhabit the land. The manitou of the Pequot Indians who died at Missituck lives in spring blooms and in the silver crystals of winter ice. Their spirits are in the rustle of the wind and in the rich loam of the ground. When each man and woman honors the manitou, it will be impossible to hate and impossible to kill without hating and killing oneself. I resolved to live like the natives, at one with all upon the earth.

Finally, grace had found me.

Oak leaves trembled in a chilly breeze even though the sun was high overhead. After a few moments I heard a rustle. Then I saw movement. I reached for my sling, thinking I might get a squirrel. But it was no squirrel.

Ayaks was not wearing war paint. He had tied back his hair into a queue the way the English wore it, and he was wearing a soft leather shirt over his buckskin pants. Around his neck was a shell necklace.

My necklace.

When he saw me, he climbed to the low branch of a tree and perched there, his eyes fixed on me. The anger was gone.

I got up and walked toward him. Slowly. Carefully. I stood under him, his moccasins next to my shoulder. He lifted the necklace and dangled it in the air for a moment. Then he lowered it toward me. I took his hand and pulled him from the limb. He landed with a soft thud inches from me. My heart was trying to tear itself from my body.

Ayaks put the necklace around my neck and pulled me toward him. His lips touched my forehead. Yes, this was right. It was as if we had reached back through time and found each other after centuries apart. I would not let him walk away from me again.

He kissed each of my eyes, barely touching my lids, his fingers in my hair. Such pleasure filled me that I had to hold back laughter. I raised my face to his, and when our lips touched, I felt his sorrow flow into me and with it, his forgiveness.

"Come," I said, and I led Ayaks back to our cart. He helped John tie down our bundles. It pleased me to see them together, almost like brothers. Ayaks tightened the rope and John knotted it. They clapped each other on the back, good-natured.

"Running Wolf," Ayaks said.

John grinned.

I sniffed the aroma of the brook that babbled by the road, clean and innocent. At the top of a tree a thrush sang its flute-like notes, a joyful yearning, calling to its mate. Ruby snorted in the pen. The ox was too old now to work but had served us well in helping to establish a civilization in the wilderness. I was older, too, so much older and wiser.

When Richard came again from the house, I froze.

"What's the meaning of this?" he said.

I would not be cowed by my brother.

"Richard, please—" I rubbed my hands on my skirt, the threads drying my palms. Richard had no musket or sword. If he came at Ayaks, it would be man to man.

I looked at Ayaks, who stood his ground, shoulders back, head high, proud even though his family had been torn from him and his father had abandoned him to the Pequot. As I saw it, Ayaks had two choices—slavery at the hands of the Narrangansett or living among the English. The English who hated him. The English destroyers of his people. But we could be his people— John and I—if Ayaks wished it.

Richard's hands were curled into fists at his sides. I stood between them, my brother and his enemy. I had to choose, and I had to do it now.

I stepped toward Richard.

"I will miss you." I wrapped my arms around his shoulders. "Wish us well, Richard. Wish all three of us well."

I felt Richard's hands on my back, his palms flat. He heaved a sigh.

When I let him go, his eyes were fixed on Ayaks. There was no longer hostility on his face.

"Give us your blessing," I said. Richard knew me well enough to understand that I would not move from this spot until he yielded.

A drum beat in my chest. Tree leaves slapped each other. In the brook water rattled a stone over rocks. Then slowly Richard nodded at Ayaks. His blessing.

When we walked away from Hartford, I wasn't thinking about what would happen when we arrived in Boston. We had a fortnight of travel ahead of us, and the path was dappled with sunlight.

ACKNOWLEDGMENTS

According to "Mystic Voices" on the Pequot War website, the annihilation of the Pequot tribal people in 1636 lifted the last major obstacle in the way of European domination in the New World. As settlements expanded, suppression of natives continued. Many Native Americans believe the subjugation that began with the Pequot War and the concept of Manifest Destiny echoes to this day.

I am indebted to my father-in-law Stephen Parson who set the wheels in motion for this story with ancestry research for his own book titled *An American Family: The Lymans and the Vale, 1631 to 1951*. With his permission, I took the seeds of the Lyman beginnings in America and nurtured them into this fictional tale. Although the incidents around the characters are factually based, the events took life from my own imagination.

Dozens of books and websites were used to extract details of seventeenth century life, including *Customs and Fashions in Old New England* and *Curious Punishments of Bygone Days* by Alice Morse Earle, *Folk Medicines* by D. C. Jarvis, and *The Puritan Family* by Edmund Morgan. The Mashantucket Pequot Museum and Research Center in

Mashantucket, Connecticut, was a valuable resource for bringing the Pequot people and their culture to light. Sandy McCall was kind enough to give me a copy of Chaucer's *Canterbury Tales* with modern interpretation of the old English. My careful readers have been my guides: Sally Baldwin, Ann Kensek, Shannon Anton, Jacqueline Tuxill, Harriet Szanto, Sarah McGrath, Stephanie Miraglia, and Michelle Fornier Houghton. Thanks go to my editor Reagan Rothe and David King at Black Rose Writing for helping make this manuscript what it needed to be. And a hundred thanks to my husband Harrison Reynolds for his patience and endless encouragement as I wrote this book.

FOR FURTHER STUDY

Seventeenth century piracy on the Atlantic

King Charles I of England and the divine right of kings

Early eastern Native American tribes, their territories and allegiances

Early American weapons and their uses

Early American folk medicines

Early American punishments and their ethics by today's standards

Early American dating patterns, especially among Puritans

Rebellion and separation as a natural consequence of growing up

The role of women in the American colonies

Colonial foods

The influence of Governor Winthrop on Massachusetts

The influence of Thomas Hooker on Connecticut

Events leading to the 1636-37 Pequot War

Manifest Destiny

Stories in your own family heritage.

ABOUT THE AUTHOR

Louella Bryant is an award-winning author of four novels of historical fiction, a biography of the Vietnam era set in Australia, a memoir, and a collection of stories, as well as short stories, poems, and essays appearing in anthologies and magazines. Currently she is an independent editor living in rural Vermont.

Visit her webpage at
http://louellabryant.com

NOTE FROM THE AUTHOR

Word-of-mouth is crucial for any author to succeed. If you enjoyed *Beside the Long River*, please leave a review online — anywhere you are able. Even if it's just a sentence or two. It would make all the difference and would be very much appreciated.

Thanks!
Louella Bryant

We hope you enjoyed reading this title from:

www.blackrosewriting.com

Subscribe to our mailing list – *The Rosevine* – and receive **FREE** books, daily deals, and stay current with news about upcoming releases and our hottest authors.

Scan the QR code below to sign up.

Already a subscriber? Please accept a sincere thank you for being a fan of Black Rose Writing authors.

View other Black Rose Writing titles at www.blackrosewriting.com/books and use promo code **PRINT** to receive a **20% discount** when purchasing.

Made in the USA
Monee, IL
27 January 2024

52307865R00111